"I want you in my bed, Diana."

She ran her hand over the rough bristles of hay. "Well, unless your name is Little Boy Blue, I'd guess this isn't it. I thought haystacks were supposed to be fluffy piles of soft, yellow stuff."

Brock raised his head and grinned down at her. "Since the invention of the baler, rolling in the hay ain't what it used to be."

The horizon suddenly lit up, and Diana propped herself on her elbows. "What was that?"

"Heat lightning." He sat up with a sigh. "Which means we'd better get down from here before it curls our hair."

It happened again—jagged white etchings snaking silently across the sky. Diana was transfixed. "I didn't hear any thunder."

"It's heat lightning," he repeated as he offered her a hand. "It sneaks up on you without a sound." He gave her a quick, hard, highly charged kiss. "But it's dangerous."

"Electrifying," she whispered.

Now and Forever

KATHLEEN EAGLE

Heat Lightning

PAGEANT BOOKS

PAGEANT BOOKS
225 Park Avenue South
New York, New York 10003

PAGEANT and colophon are trademarks of the publisher

NOW AND FOREVER is a trademark of Mega–Books of New York, Inc.

Cover artwork by Renato Aime

Printed in the U.S.A.

First Pageant Books printing: March, 1989

10 9 8 7 6 5 4 3 2 1

For Christopher
happy birthday

Chapter One

She'd been driving for hours. Diana was giddy with fatigue when a silly line from a poem floated across her mind along with the big blue balloon that drifted suddenly in front of her car. "The goat-footed old balloon man whistled far and whee . . ." Then she caught sight of the small figure, the white shirt, the little hand reaching toward the trailing string.

Tires skidded and brakes screeched as the car jolted to a stop. Diana was unsure of the precise moves that her reflexes had prompted. Draped over the steering wheel, eyes closed, body trembling, she knew only that there was a small boy in front of her car . . . or under it. When she raised her head and blinked at the windshield, two huge brown eyes peered back at her. There was no mouth, no chin—only the eyes peeking over the hood of the car.

It took some presence of mind to kick the parking brake before she threw open the door and scrambled out of the car, dropping to her knees in front of the child.

"Are you all right? Did the car hit you? Where's your mother? What are you doing in the road? Don't you—"

The child's squalling outburst made more sense than

Diana's own. She looked at the hands that shook his little shoulders and was amazed to find that they were hers.

"Chris! Chris!" The screaming boy was snatched from her grip, and pulled into the arms of a tall man.

Diana stared at the stranger who towered above her, his head and shoulders etched against the clear blue sky. She heard the voice, soothing in its deep, even tone, telling the boy that he was okay. Soon the crying abated to a hiccuping whimper. Diana's nerves responded to the voice, and she grabbed her own shoulders, arms crossed over her chest to still the trembling.

"It's okay, Chris. She didn't mean to scare you. See? You scared her, too." The man leaned down, the child riding his left hip, and tried to help Diana up. She responded mechanically, her eyes searching his face through her tears.

He was surprised to discover she was shaking. "No harm done, ma'am. None that I can see, anyway."

"He—he just appeared out of nowhere. First the balloon—then the boy . . ."

"Balloon must've gotten away from him. It was close, but you slammed on those brakes in time, thank God." The man gave Diana a harder look. "*You* okay, ma'am?"

"I might have killed him." She couldn't stop trembling, couldn't focus her eyes or her thoughts.

"You stopped in time, though. That's all that counts."

"What counts is that I almost killed him! He was out in the road, and I almost ran over him!" Jerking her shoulder away from him to free her arm, Diana spun on her heel and marched to the roadside.

"Hey, lady, your car's in the middle of the road! Hey!" Dumbfounded, Brock Reed watched the woman walk away from her car and into the auto dealer's parking lot, as though she'd had enough of this car and intended to shop for a new one. Then he looked at the trim, late-model foreign job sitting cockeyed near the median.

A police car was slowing on the opposite side. "Trouble, Brock?" the officer shouted across the short distance.

Shifting the now quiet Christopher in his arm, Brock headed for the open door on the driver's side of the lady's car. "No problem, Dan. Little misunderstanding is all." Settling Christopher on the passenger's side, Brock slid onto the driver's seat and pulled into the lot, parking the little red car next to his own blue-and-silver pickup. When he climbed out of the car and looked around, there was no wild-eyed, shaking woman to be seen. He peered into the showroom window between the words "Low" and "Interest" that were painted in red on the glass. Maybe she *had* abandoned the car. Giving the red roof a reassuring pat, he muttered absently, "It wasn't your fault."

"It wasn't my fault, was it, Daddy?" Christopher had scooted behind the wheel, and his doleful expression drew a hair ruffling from the same hand that had comforted the car.

"No, son, you . . . well, in a way it was. I've told you a hundred times to stay out of the road, Chris."

"But my balloon . . ." he wailed.

"I'll get you another balloon. It wouldn't be so easy to get another Christopher." Brock reached down for his son's hand. "C'mon, let's see if that lady's okay."

"Did I scare her away?" the boy asked, stretching his toes toward the pavement as his bottom slid over the edge of the seat.

"Yeah, I think you screamed at her too loud. Women get scared when we scream at 'em."

"There she is, Daddy!"

Having composed herself to some extent in the ladies' room, Diana emerged from the showroom. She forced a smile when she saw the tall man and his little boy standing next to her car, and she strode with renewed confidence in their direction. "I'll drive you to the hospital if you like," she announced.

Brock glanced back over his shoulder and then down at the boy. "She talking to *us*, Chris? Which one of us looks like he needs a doctor?"

The boy shrugged.

"You didn't hit him, ma'am. See?" Brock laid a large, callused hand on top of the boy's head. "Not a scratch on him."

"Got this cut on a nail on the corral fence," Christopher offered, holding up his arm to let Diana see an old wound near his elbow. "Hadda get a shot already."

"Correction," Brock injected, "*one* scratch. But your car didn't even touch him, ma'am. He's fine."

"I insist we make sure, Mister . . ."

"Reed. Brock Reed. And this is Christopher, my son."

"Please, let me drive you and Christopher to the nearest hospital, Mr. Reed, just to be safe."

Brock eyed her hands, wringing one another, and still unsteady. "I'm not too sure we'd be safe with you at the wheel right now."

"I don't want to go to the doctor, Daddy." Tugging desperately at his father's pant leg, Christopher craned his neck back to give his father full view of his gathering tears and downturned little mouth. "Please, Daddy."

"Christopher," Diana began, her voice having lost some of its authoritative crispness, "let's just make certain that I didn't hurt you. The doctor won't—"

"Noooo," Christopher wailed, beginning to cry in earnest. Brock reached down and gathered the sniffling bundle into his arms.

"How about if the three of us just take a little stroll to this pop stop up ahead and calm our nerves over a cold drink?" he offered, trying to keep his tone light. What was wrong with this woman, anyway? Couldn't she see that Chris was fine—except for the fact that she was scaring the hell out of him with this hospital stuff?

"No. No, really, I—"

"Look, ma'am. You're more shaken than the kid here. Have a Coke with us. We'll just watch him, make sure he doesn't develop any delayed reactions or anything. And you can have a minute to settle down. Then you can head back to Rhode Island with a clear conscience. C'mon." He cocked his head in the direction of the big orange sign.

"Rhode Island? How did you—"

"Your plates. Just a minute," he said, looking toward the showroom. "I left my hat inside when I went tearing out the door."

"I should move my car. . . ."

"It's okay where it is. Friend of mine works here. Don't go away—I'll be right back." Brock threw the boy over his shoulder, and he and Christopher ducked back into the showroom.

He was right back, before the door had even closed behind him, settling a straw cowboy hat on top of his curly black hair and pulling Christopher along behind him. "Yeah, he's fine," Brock called back through the door to a salesman standing behind a yellow car. "No problem. See you guys later."

Diana had taken her purse from the car, and she fell into step beside him as they headed across the road. Brock glanced down at her and smiled. "What's your name, Little Rhodey?"

"Diana Daviau . . . I mean, Diana Peters. I just reclaimed my maiden name. I keep forgetting."

"Just as well you divorced him." Brock chuckled, holding the diner's door open for her. "Diana Daviau sounds like some sort of movie starlet." She threw him a disapproving glance, and he knew he'd overstepped the bounds of the newly introduced.

"How do you know I'm not?" she asked crisply.

"No sunglasses."

She pulled a pair of dark glasses from her purse and perched them on the bridge of her nose.

Brock studied the look for a moment—sun-streaked blond hair, pink top and white cotton pants, sandals, delicious figure. "Yeah, I guess you could be. But not with Rhode Island plates. Your plates would say something like 'LOVE-DD.' And they'd be issued in California. Right?" Finally she gave him a genuine smile as she lowered the glasses. "What'll it be, Diana?" he asked.

Christopher concentrated on a chocolate milkshake and Diana sipped soda through a straw while Brock drank from the cup, chewing the crushed ice left in his mouth after each swallow. "So . . . what brings you way out here to North Dakota, Miss Peters?"

"I'm here to visit friends. My college roommate and her husband farm out here. I think I'm almost there. It's west of Bismarck."

"What's the name?"

"Reinhart. Jackie and Jim."

"Oh, sure! My neighbors, about five miles down the road from me. You've got less than half an hour's drive. How long you staying?"

"I don't know. A couple of weeks or so . . . until I feel like going back," she said, allowing herself a small sigh.

"How long ago was this divorce, anyway?"

"Two years separated, two months divorced. Old news, really. Is he all right?" She was studying Christopher, who seemed to be having a spasm of some sort.

Brock looked down at the boy beside him. "Hiccups. You're drinking too fast, son. Take it slow and try to act cool. This lady's watching every move you make."

Christopher poised his mouth over the straw again, giving Diana a wary stare as he drank.

"I'm sure Christopher's mother would be on my side," Diana ventured.

"I doubt it. Christopher's mother is . . . out of the picture."

"What picture, Daddy?"

"Remember that picture you drew the other day, Chris? You and me and Jake? Mom wasn't in it, remember?"

"Yeah. I guess I forgot to draw her. I'll do it when we get back home, Daddy."

"You have custody?" Diana asked.

"Yes. She never . . . he hasn't seen her since he was two years old, but he still seems to remember."

"How old is he?"

"How old are you, Chris?" Brock prompted. The little hand went up, five fingers splayed wide.

"Five years old! You're a big boy for five," Diana said, knowing that her comment would please the child.

Christopher nodded, sucking enthusiastically at the thick shake.

"He outgrows a pair of tennis shoes every month, this kid. Gonna be as big as his dad. Right, son?"

Christopher nodded again.

"You feel quite certain he's all right, don't you?"

"I'm quite certain you didn't hit him, so I'm sure he's all right. A thing like that can really shake you up, I know, but I wish you'd put your mind at rest now. You sure you wouldn't like a drink? There's a restaurant just down the street, and—"

"No, thank you. I don't need anything to calm me down," Diana insisted almost defensively.

"Well, since you'll be staying with my neighbors, maybe you'll take a rain check." She was very attractive, this woman who'd nearly flattened his son. Not really beautiful, not like Lori had been. No, this woman had a more sophisticated, almost exotic allure. Her hair was wheat-colored, highlighted by its hot beach sun streaks. The sultry mouth was appealing, the nose nondescript. It was her eyes that drew attention. They were long-lashed, green, and almond-shaped, hinting of a face that should have been draped with a veil. He wondered what that shapely body would look like in harem pants with teasing tassels and floats of silk.

"I don't know what Jackie has planned for me, but, yes, I'd like that."

"You live near the ocean?" Brock asked.

"Yes, Newport. Why?"

"It shows. I wouldn't be surprised to see you shake some sand out of your shoes."

"You've been around beach towns?"

"Some. I was in the navy."

"Ah. And now you . . . farm?"

"A little farming. Mostly cattle ranching. Reinharts *ranch,* by the way. They don't *farm.* You've gotta watch that around here. There's a difference."

"I'm sure I'll spend the next couple of weeks finding out what the difference is."

"And what do you do, Diana Peters?"

"I'm a lawyer."

One eyebrow cocked over one dark eye, almost in disbelief. "A lady lawyer?"

"I believe so. My birth certificate says female, and I am most assuredly a member of the bar. Don't you have any *lady* lawyers in North Dakota?"

"Sure, I guess so. Don't know any myself, but then I haven't been keeping up with the news lately. Could be you got the vote, for all I know."

"Have I stumbled into a genuine bastion of male chauvinism? Maybe I could find a good sex discrimination case while I'm here."

"No, I guess women are pretty liberated here—free to come and go as they please. Mine did, anyway."

There was an awkward moment of silence before Diana said, "I'd better be on my way before Jackie sends out a posse. I called her just before I . . . just before Christopher and I almost ran into each other."

"No more posses. We've got real police cars—one of which stopped to check out the little red car that was left in the middle of the road a while ago."

"Oh, I . . . Thank you for moving it. I don't know why I did that. I was—"

"Pretty shook up. I should've been watching him closer. I got to talking to somebody, and he—"

"Daddy, don't forget. You said you'd get me another balloon," Christopher reminded him.

"We'll tie the next one to your belt, Chris. Tell you what, Diana. You follow me, and I'll lead you right to the Reinharts' doorstep."

"Not unless you've finished your business here."

"All done. Ready, Chris?"

Jackie and Jim Reinhart live in an L-shaped ranch-style home almost three miles off the main highway along a gravel road. Diana saw Brock point to the "Reinhart" sign marking the driveway. Tooting his pickup horn, he waved and sped down the road, leaving a billowing cloud of dust in his wake.

Jackie flew out the back door even before Diana shut off the engine. "Did you get lost? I was frantic. There's a maze of gravel roads around here," Jackie exclaimed, but her smiling eyes told Diana that she was delighted to see her old friend.

Arms around each other's waists, they headed for the back step, Diana explaining the delay and apologizing for the worry she'd caused.

"Well, so much for my chance to play matchmaker." Jackie sighed, her blue eyes sparkling. "I'd planned to introduce you to North Dakota's most panted-after bachelor myself. Isn't he gorgeous?"

"Jackie," Diana warned, "I'm not here to be fixed up with some cowboy. Don't start thinking that a man like Jim is just what I need to cure all my ills."

"What do you need right now? A good cup of tea?" She was already putting on the kettle while Diana sank onto a vinyl-cushioned kitchen chair.

"Yes, and a good friend—one who remembers the good old days."

"Do you want to tell your good friend about all your ills?"

"Lord, no, let's not get morbid already. Let's talk about the good old days."

"Let's talk about your trip first. How was it?"

Diana watched her friend move efficiently from cupboard to sink to stove to drawer. Jackie seemed to have everything so together. Diana wondered if she herself could put a teacup together with the right saucer at this point. "It was long."

"Why didn't you fly?"

"I didn't want to. I wanted to have my own wheels. I needed to feel in control."

Jackie laughed. "I've never known you *not* to be in control, Diana. You've always had everything down on schedule with the proper aplomb."

"Ah, yes, *those* were the good old days. I handled school that way, and law school, and my legal practice. But my personal life is another matter entirely."

"You had a well-organized start," Jackie observed, delivering the cups of tea to the table and sitting down. "You had Doug all picked out and on your agenda years ahead of time."

"He should have been the right choice, too. All the signs were compatible. We were the perfect couple . . . until Robbie came along."

"I'm so sorry about the baby, Diana."

"We'll talk about it later, okay? One of these nights over a bottle of wine. Remember how we used to analyze everybody, solve all the world's problems, make all our most serious plans?"

"I remember." Jackie's eyes softened. "I remember the time we walked back to the dorm—it was one of those quiet winter nights—and you shouted to the treetops that I was your best friend. It was so unlike you. Do you know how special that made me feel? The little hick from North Dakota singled out like the North Star."

It was Diana's turn to laugh. "I'd never had a best friend before. That was a great moment—a wonderful discovery. The future was a blinding brightness just then."

"It was all so simple, wasn't it? So incredibly clear. We had great plans, and there was never any question that we would accomplish everything we set out to do, was there?"

Diana lifted her eyebrows in assent. *Such memories. Such memories.* "And did you, Jackie? Where's your model rural school—Jackie Henderson, teacher, principal, janitor, and bus driver?"

"I taught for a while, but I never got my rural school. Jim and Jeff and Tracy keep me busy, and this is what I want right now."

"And I have Johnson, Myers, Hopkins, Hopkins, and . . . Peters. They just changed the sign." Diana was distant for a moment, and then a shadow of fear crept into her eyes. "Jackie, I nearly flipped out today when I thought I'd hit that little boy."

"You were lucky. . . ."

"Lucky? *He* was lucky. *I* was half-crazy! When I saw him standing there looking surprised and . . . so little, I just wanted to paddle his bottom. But then I was so relieved, I wanted to hug him and thank him for not being dead. And when the father got there, I wanted to slap him for letting that child out of his sight. But I should have thanked him for not slapping me. I almost killed that little boy, Jackie."

"For heaven's sake, Diana, you're taking a lot of blame for a freak accident that you managed to avoid."

"Sometimes I wonder whether I'm still playing with a full deck. Do you know what I did? I left my car sitting there in the road. That man had to move it for me."

"Where did you go?"

"I didn't know where I was going. I found myself in the ladies' room of the closest building, which was an auto dealer's."

"And when you came out, you were Miss Diana Peters again—composed, self-assured—"

"A nervous wreck. I went with them to get something to drink. I'm not even sure why I went, except that I wanted to see that the boy was really all right."

"And because Brock Reed is a charming and genuinely considerate man who wanted to be sure that *you* were all right."

"Don't start trying to plant the seeds of something, Jackie." Diana sipped her tea, wanting to put the topic to rest.

"Brock's not just a pretty face. He's a good man to have for a friend," Jackie testified.

She should have known that Jackie wouldn't give up that easily. "How did he get custody of the boy? Pretty unusual for a two-year-old to go to the father."

"His wife left him—left both of them. Brock was in school at the time."

"In school? He must be younger than I thought."

"No, he's our age—a little older—early thirties. He worked on the family ranch for a while after high school. Then he joined the navy—mostly to get away, I think. Met Lori in California somewhere. She never liked it here. Brock went to school after he got out of the navy. He had the GI Bill, worked, struggled like all married students. Lori had the decency to wait until his last year before she took off, so he did graduate. I guess with the baby to take care of, it was easier to come back home and work with the ranch again. His mother's moved into town now."

"Well," Diana admitted, "Brock was very civil— considering that I nearly mowed down his son."

"Civil?" Jackie echoed. "Try *gorgeous.*"

"He . . . suggested we might go out for a drink some-time," Diana said casually. "If he calls, I think I'll go."

"Good. He'll show you a good time. Though North Dakota night life is a little different from what you're used to."

"No doubt. But I can tolerate one evening for the sake of your matchmaking compulsion, old roomy of mine."

Chapter Two

Two days later, it rained.

"Di-an-a, you're wanted on the pho-one," Jackie sang out, handing over the receiver with a canary-was-delicious grin.

"Hi," said the low, mellow male voice. "How about cashing in our rain check tonight?"

"Haven't you got it backward? A rain check is supposed to be good when the weather improves."

"You're in farm country now, lady. This is good weather. We make hay while the sun shines, literally. When it rains, I get to play. You're not busy tonight. I already checked with your hostess. Dinner for two?"

"What about Christopher?"

"I'm dumping him off on Jackie. I checked that out, too. Six okay?"

"That's not exactly the dinner hour."

"It is here. I'll be starving by then. Be ready, okay?"

"I'll see what I can do."

Diana made it her habit to be punctual, but Brock was fifteen minutes early. At precisely six o'clock she entered the living room wearing a blue silk dress with a draped

15

neckline, sashed at her small waist. The hemline floated around her legs with feminine grace.

Yes, Brock thought, pleased that she had dressed up for him, *silk becomes her*.

"I'm sorry I kept you waiting, Brock. But you . . ." He stood by the fireplace with Jim, both sipping on bottles of beer. Every inch the cowboy, he wore a blue print western shirt, his wheat-color western-cut pants riding low at the base of a long waist. "You were a bit early."

A slow smile spread across his face, pure pleasure reflected in his eyes. "You look great, Little Rhodey."

"I . . . thank you. But I seem to be overdressed."

"No, you wouldn't want to wear much less. No shoes, no shirt, no service. We're real fussy here."

She refused to groan. "I could change if—"

"Hell, no, lady, I've waited long enough!" He drained his beer and crossed the distance between them. "And, as I said, you look great. I'm taking you to a fancy place— worthy of your silk dress. What do you think of East Forty, Jim?" Brock's eyes did not leave Diana as he spoke.

"Good choice," Jim responded from the far end of the room.

"I even brought a jacket," Brock added with a wink. "Can't guarantee I'll put it on, but I got it as far as the pickup."

"Pickup?" Diana glanced down at her dress again.

"Hey, it's clean. *Inside,* anyway. Worked on that this afternoon. Polished my boots, took a bath, got ready for the big city. Left my chew at home, too. Figure that might bother you."

"Chew?"

Jackie's giggle announced her presence in the room.

"Oh, Brock, you don't chew. Stop teasing Diana, now, or she might send you and your pickup back where you came from."

"And break my little pea-pickin' heart? This lady's got too much class for that. She'll shore up her patience and be discreet about seeing that I get through dinner on the right fork. Won't you, Diana?"

"Is this all part of some initiation rite for eastern city slickers?" Diana asked, her smile frankly flirting.

"Hell, no. The initiation comes when we work cows."

"Tell me, do you ever say 'no' without prefacing it with the word 'hell'?"

Brock glanced at Jackie, who raised her eyebrows to indicate that he'd been forewarned. Turning back to Diana, he admitted, "I don't know. Probably on rare occasions. If we spend some time together, maybe you can improve my vocabulary."

"And maybe you can add some color to mine."

They eyed each other for a moment. The attraction between them was almost tangible, underscored by the momentary silence in the room.

"Christopher's out in the yard with Jeff," Jackie said. "He can stay the night, Brock."

"You sure it's no trouble?"

"Jeff has it all planned. They're going to camp out in the living room. Pull your pickup into the garage so Diana won't have to go out in the rain."

"Diana? What about me?"

"The water'll roll right off your back," Jackie teased him. "Anyway, it looks like it's beginning to clear."

The restaurant was decorated in prairie antiques. They were seated in a cozy, curtained booth, which enveloped them in a quiet little world of their own. It occurred to Diana that she hardly knew this man, but she felt completely comfortable in his company. She had spent a lifetime planning everything—her feelings, her friendships, her future—and she was beginning to realize why it hadn't always worked. She could never have planned Brock Reed. His easy smile and the smooth flow of their conversation came naturally, and even though the food was good, she hardly noticed what she ate. She simply enjoyed it.

"So tell me," Brock began, lifting his glass for a sip of wine. "What is it like to be a lawyer?"

"A *lady* lawyer?"

"No point in telling me what it's like to be a lady. That I'll have to imagine from the other side of the hormones. What's it like to be a lawyer?"

"I'm a very junior member of a very highly regarded law firm. It's what I've always wanted, and I enjoy it very much."

"That's three *very*'s. Must be a good job. Are you good at it?"

"Of course. I'm thorough, efficient, organized—I know my stuff."

"Ever had any . . . child custody cases?"

"Yes, quite a few."

"Ever represent the man?"

"Several times."

"Ever get his kid for him?"

Diana swirled the wine in her glass, watching her reflection as she said, "I've never been able to get full custody for the father, but then they don't usually sue for full custody." She looked up, offering frankly, "You were very lucky to get that, Brock. Apparently your wife didn't contest it."

"Not so far. She just wanted out."

"If she changes her mind, even at this late date, you might have to share him. Of course, I know nothing of the circumstances. . . ."

"That'll never happen." He tipped the glass to his mouth and swallowed three times before adding, "I'd take my boy to Tasmania before I'd let her get her hands on him."

This was getting too heavy. "How's the ranching in Tasmania?"

"I don't know." He smiled, and the worry lines disappeared from his face. "I'm not even sure where the hell Tasmania is. Must be east of Rhode Island. . . . Ever do any dancing?"

"Occasionally."

"Are you good at it?"

"Of course. Thorough, efficient . . ."

"And you know your stuff. So do I." He tossed some bills on the table and slid out of the booth. "Let's see if we can get our stuff together, Miss Peters."

Getting in and out of the pickup was tricky for Diana, requiring a gentleman's assistance. Brock grinned as he helped her down, commenting that it was just like the carriages of old. "Instant romance," he called it, and Diana realized that she liked the way his hand lingered at her waist after her feet were on the ground. He smelled of wine and some woodsy men's cologne, and the nearness of him gave her a buoyant feeling, a feeling she hadn't encountered for years.

There were unmasked stares for the attractive couple as they made their way past the lounge's dance floor in search of an empty table. Brock greeted several people on the way and managed to find a table that was out of the amplifiers' direct blast.

While Brock drank beer, Diana sipped another glass of wine, both waiting for the right song before they took to the dance floor. Then they danced, each enjoying thoroughly the way the other moved to the lively country-rock beat. When Brock guided her back to the table, his hand resting at the small of her back, Diana was smiling for no particular reason.

"Hey, Brock, where'd you disappear to the other day?" Turning slightly in her chair, Diana found two women hovering over the table.

"I'm sorry, Rita," Brock offered. "Something came up, and I had to take off. Diana, this is Rita Hatch and her friend. . . ."

"Melanie," Rita supplied. "I thought we had a date, Brock. You never said a word. I waited—"

"I guess I just forgot, Rita. I'm sorry." Brock grinned sheepishly, trying to complete his introductions as though that amenity would make up for past mistakes. "Rita works at Richardson's, the car dealer where I ran into you the other day. Rita, this is Diana—"

"I waited until after closing, thinking we had a date." An attractive blonde, Rita was dressed for a manhunt, and her voice left no doubt that she was determined to close in on this quarry. "I'd already arranged to take off early and everything. What'd you do, pick up one of the customers?"

"It . . . must've been my fault," Diane attempted.

"Something came up, Rita. It was *my* fault, and all I can say is, I'm sorry."

Rita's eyes narrowed, but she gave Brock a cocked hip and a saucy smile. "Listen, you big bastard farmer, that's the second time in a week you've stood me up. I ought to swear out a complaint against you.''

"I think you just did. You'll have to excuse us, Rita. Diana promised me this dance.''

Diana peeked around Brock's shoulder as he settled his arm around her waist. Rita glowered back at her, sipped deeply on her beer, then moved away from the table. "Are you really such a cad, Brock?''

"As far as I know, my birth was legitimate. I'm a rancher more than a farmer, and I didn't stand her up the first time; I called to say I couldn't make it.''

"I don't think you're going to get a chance at a third strike.''

"Rita's really pretty easygoing. Bet she'll even pitch me a walk next time.''

"Her bases seem to be pretty loaded right now. Sure you don't want to try for a grand slam? I'll retire my side.''

Brock's eyes danced with delight. "Her game got rained out.''

"But your social life only flourishes in the rain.''

"It flourishes when I want it to—when an interesting lady is interested in me.'' His hand crept along her waist to find a tender spot, and he held her near him. "Like right now.''

"Are you sure both conditions exist right now?''

"Damn sure,'' he answered with a punctuating wink.

His point was made as the evening progressed. Diana found his conversation as stimulating as the fluid way he moved his body when they danced. The slower the music, the closer he held her, until their hips swayed against each other and she rested her temple against the square line of his jaw.

Brock had waited for her to move closer, feeling her relax as she inched toward him. Enjoying her response, he slowly tightened the slack in his right arm. Front to front, they brushed each other with tickling, shivering sensations. Her hair had a still-fresh citrus scent, and he breathed in deeply, savoring it. As he closed his eyes and envisioned swaying fruit trees and two round breasts and blossom-petal soft skin, he drew her firmly against him, pressing his lips along the hairline at her temple. His light kiss caused a small but gratifying catch in her breath.

When the music stopped, neither wanted to make the move to step away from the other.

"Getting pretty smoky in here," Brock mumbled. "Why don't we find some fresh air?"

Outside, the night air was clear, and Diana could smell the damp cleanliness of it. Brock helped her into the pickup and then slid behind the wheel.

"Kind of nice sitting up this high," she remarked. "You can look down on all the other cars. You know, I don't think I've ridden in one of these but maybe once or twice in my life."

"Ever driven a tractor?"

"No. I don't think I know any tractor owners at home."

"Good. That puts me in an interesting category—the only guy you know with a pickup and a tractor. Let's see . . . what else have I got to dazzle you with? How 'bout stars?"

"Other guys have shown me stars."

"Not like mine. No moon tonight, but I'll save that for another time. Let me show you a North Dakota sky at night."

Brock pointed the pickup uphill on a gravel road west of town. As they neared the top of the road, he whistled softly, slamming on the brakes and securing the vehicle.

"I'll be damned." He flashed a grin at Diana. "This must be a sign from heaven. Celestial approval of our first date." He hopped out and reached for her to follow on his side. "Hurry, before it fades away."

Curious, Diana scooted under the wheel and let Brock lower her to the ground. They walked the short distance to the top, Diana indeed dazzled by the spectacle that surrounded the hilltop and covered the arc of the heavens.

"What is it?" she breathed. What had seemed in the first seconds to be a faint illusion of a fractured midnight rainbow was now growing brighter. The colors were translucent, and the light intensified in prismatic shafts, bobbing like horses on a carousel that circumscribed the horizon of the prairie.

"Northern lights. Ever seen 'em before?"

"No, no, never . . . my God! It's like magic!" She shivered, whether from the cool breeze on her bare arms or from sheer awe, she didn't know.

"Cold?" Brock stepped close behind her, blocking the hilltop breeze. She didn't answer. He settled his hands at the tops of her arms and, finding her skin cool to the touch, slid them up and down several times to create warm friction. When she leaned against his chest in response, he draped the burly shawl of his arms around her shoulders.

"Does this happen often?" she asked, trying to take it all in with wide eyes.

"No, only when conditions are . . . just right." He rested his cheek against her hair.

"What conditions?"

"Atmospheric, I guess. When the positive is accentuated and the negative is . . . eliminated." With guarded discretion, he nuzzled the citrusy softness.

"How can it happen in the summer? I thought—"

"It can happen any time, Diana—generally when it's least expected. You look up and all of a sudden your whole body feels like it's shot through with light." He turned her in his arms, and she gazed up at him, the spectacle of light dancing behind his head.

She hadn't realized how hard her heart was pounding until she saw those dark eyes. They seemed to look deep into her brain and demand an accelerated pulse rate.

"You see what I mean, don't you." There was no question in his voice.

"Brock . . ."

"Atmospheric conditions tolerate only the positive at this moment. The negative has been eliminated."

As she watched the descent of his mouth, she knew that he was right. Tilting her head, she welcomed his kiss, her lips falling open to permit the tentative flicker of his tongue at the portal of her mouth. Eyes closed, arms stretched around the expanse of his back, Diana still saw the lights, teeter-tottering like glowing pistons, setting an erratic pace for her respiratory system. His body was hard and warm, and she melted against him. His tongue grew bolder, his lips demanding more response, and she groaned—a small, defenseless, willing groan—as she answered with the darting caress of her own tongue.

"Brock," she whispered again when his lips moved reluctantly from hers. There was new expression in the pronouncement this time.

"Bright lights . . . beautiful, bright lights," he murmured before making a second positive impression on her mouth.

Chapter Three

"What can I do to help, Jackie? I'll tell you right now, I'm worthless when it comes to baking, but I'm told my baked beans are unbeatable, and I'm pretty good with potato salad."

"We'll make a good team, then. I hate making potato salad. I warn you, though, we're talking gallons here."

"How many people do you expect tomorrow, anyway? This is enough bread for the sojourn in the wilderness." Diana lifted her chin in the direction of the heaps of fresh buns as she reached into the bin of potatoes.

"You never know who might bring half a dozen extra friends along. When we have a barbecue, Jim just spreads around an open invitation. Most of the men'll get here early to help Jim round up and work cows. They'll have that done by noon. I know one neighbor I can count on for sure." Jackie grinned in Diana's direction. "He said he'd be here early. Wondered if you knew how to ride."

"Horseback?"

"Of course, horseback. Brock usually brings over several of his horses when he helps us work cows. We only have three saddle horses."

"I guess I can still sit a horse. It's been years, though. Where's your vegetable brush?" The instrument in question was produced, and Diana leaned over the sink to scrub potatoes.

"He likes you, Diana."

"I guess I'm likable enough," Diana said offhandedly.

"I mean he *really* likes you."

"Jackie, I've only seen the man twice. He hardly seems the type to be readily smitten, and I'm certainly not."

"But you like him, too."

"Yes, of course I *like* him. What is this—back to adolescence? Are we making our lists of the boys we like?"

Jackie shrugged. "I'm just glad you two hit it off so well."

"This paring knife would be just the thing to clip those Cupid wings back a little," Diana warned, waving her weapon with a smile.

"No matter. I've already shot my arrows."

Morning light was just a haze when Jackie's head craned around the door of the guest room. "Better jump into your jeans, Diana. Brock just pulled in."

Diana lifted one eyelid and peered over her pillow. "What an ungodly hour to start the day," she groaned.

"Hurry up. After he gets the horses unloaded, he'll be in here for coffee. You don't want to look like you just got out of bed."

"I don't?"

"Come on, Diana, you've got ten minutes to put on a happy face," Jackie urged as she shut the door.

Reluctantly Diana dropped her legs over the side of the bed and propped her body in an upright position. Ten minutes, did she say? Forget it. It would take a shower to get the blood circulating and makeup to make the face presentable. But at this hour, "happy" would be pushing it.

Diana managed a civil, if not cheery "Good morning, Brock," when she came into the kitchen a record fifteen minutes later.

"Hey, Diana! You ready to punch some cows this morning?"

His bright-eyed grin was almost insufferable. "I was ready to punch the alarm clock this morning, until I recognized it as my best friend." Diana and a pot of fresh coffee arrived at the table at the same time. She poured herself a cup and lifted it to her lips, inhaling appreciatively. "I should have volunteered to be part of the relief crew. I don't really start functioning until around nine."

"Ever do any riding?"

Diana lowered the coffee cup slowly, giving Brock one pointedly arched eyebrow and a sigh of strained patience. "I did not just recently crawl out from under an inner-city cement slab, Mr. Reed. 'Ever drive a tractor? Ever do any dancing? Ever ride a horse?' Yes, I've done some riding!"

"Diana, you said—" Jackie tried.

"As a matter of fact, I once owned my own horse."

Brock's grin had a suspiciously satisfied tilt. "What'd you put in this coffee, Jackie? She's wide wake, coiled up, and ready to strike."

"A little something to keep her one step ahead of you. And you'd better give her a gentle horse, too."

"No need to make a fuss over me. I'm sure that any animal Brock owns is quite gentle," Diana said, throwing out the gauntlet with a look of assurance, "and easy to ride."

"Your mount is saddled and ready to go. You'll like her. She hardly ever bucks," Brock promised.

"And I hardly ever strike."

The job called for the riders to roust cows and calves out of the coulees, draws, and windbreaks, bunch them up, and drive them home. Diana found that sitting a horse was like riding a bicycle: it came back after the initial reacquaintance.

As she and Brock had been assigned part of the pasture, she tried to follow his instructions. The growing bunch of cattle was herded in the general direction of home, while every hill and draw had to be checked along the way. Diana's job was to keep the herd together, but the sun felt so glorious and the openness of the land was so awesome that her attention strayed—and so did the cattle. Brock brought in a trio of cows and found three more wandering from the bunch.

"I'm sorry." She offered him a contrite smile. "They refuse to listen to me."

"You're doing fine. What do you think of the mare?"

"Very smooth . . . and very gentle."

"If you haven't ridden in a while, you're going to be sore later."

"I belong to a health club—get a lot of exercise. I'm in good physical shape."

His eyes traveled a predictable route: face-breasts-hips-breasts-face. "I'll say."

"And you're no slouch yourself." She was smiling, giving him a look that appraised his own well-proportioned anatomy.

"Why don't we go down to the river and watch the frogs catch flies? The hell with the cows," Brock suggested, the merriment in his eyes making the idea very tempting.

"No, I'm determined to ride triumphantly into that yard herding a huge bunch of these bovine brats."

"Have it your way. I'll stay with the herd this time while you check the other side of that hill. See that cowpath? Follow that across the creek."

Diana scanned the prairie in the direction indicated by his long, brown arm. She saw the cutbank, which housed the creek, the cowpath, and the low rise beyond.

"I'll be pushing west along the creek. Just take a quick look and bring along anything you find," he instructed. She nodded before she kneed her horse in the direction of the cowpath.

She had to take it slowly. She didn't want to admit it, but her legs were beginning to feel like jelly, and she felt herself coming unglued at the canter. There were no cows within sight on the other side of the hill, but she took a few moments to make certain.

Returning to the other side of the rise, she took a westerly diagonal route back to the creek, hoping to intercept Brock on the other side. She didn't see him when she reached the creek, nor did she see any cowpath. Making her way along the edge of the cutbank, Diana surveyed the creek. It was probably no more than ten or twelve feet wide. Surely she could cross anywhere along here.

At a place where the bank sloped enough for the horse to pick its way across, Diana headed down the twenty-foot embankment. The water looked almost still, but the mare hesitated. Diana urged insistently until the horse took two steps into the water and plunged on the third to withers depth.

"Oh! . . . Ooooh!" Shock came first, then fear. Diana

floated out of the saddle and grabbed for the bank, her legs scrambling in the water. She found footing, clutched at the promise of dry ground, and heaved herself over the bank.

She stumbled to her feet, relieved that she still held the reins in her hand. Backing up the grade, she turned to the mare, whose body nearly spanned the breadth of the creek. "Come on, girl. Come on. . . ."

The mare gave it a try, but there was little for her to brace her weight on. She fell back in, seeming to sink even farther into the water.

"Oh, no, girl, don't! You can do it. Come on . . . try again." Something sensible in her brain told Diana to stay calm, speak softly. "You knew better than to try it here, didn't you? I should have listened to you. Try again, girl, you can do it."

After another futile attempt, the mare sank even lower, her mane floating like brown seawood on the surface of the water, her nostrils flaring just above the waterline.

"Oh, no, you can't. . . . Brock!" she screamed. "Brock, help me!" She screamed and screamed until her throat was raw. Then she heard the pounding of hooves above her.

"Diana! Diana!" His face, blessedly, appeared over the edge of the cutbank.

"Brock, help me! She's going to drown!"

Brock skidded down the embankment on his boot heels. "It's okay, Diana. She'll find her footing." He took the reins and led the horse downstream a short distance. Suddenly she lunged out of the water and up on dry land, her powerful hindquarters propelling her to the top of the cutbank as Brock released the rein.

Taking several ground-eating strides, Brock came back to Diana's side. "You all right?" His hands gripped her shoulders, and he held her at arm's length, looking for damage. "Okay?" he asked again.

Diana nodded dumbly.

"I shouldn't have sent you across the creek. I thought you'd . . . I guess I didn't think."

"Who'd have thought such a narrow stream could be so deep?" she asked in a small voice.

"These creeks can run pretty deep on the flat. God, I'm sorry, Diana. Were you . . . did you have trouble getting out?"

"No. I was afraid I'd lose the horse, though."

"Well, now look at you, Little Rhodey. You're all wet." He surveyed her more casually this time.

"Yes . . . I'm all wet." She looked at herself, then at Brock, whose mouth was twitching at the corners.

The laughter burst from both of them at the same time. He took her by the hand and pulled her up the embankment. "I borrowed these boots from Jackie," Diana said. "I hope they're not ruined."

"They've seen their share of mud and manure, I'm sure. God, you were a sorry sight."

"Were?"

"Are. So much for your triumphant return."

Diana was amazed that the mare stood grazing quietly at the top of the ledge—she'd've been within her rights to hightail it home in disgust. And at this point Diana herself might be more comfortable walking.

But she dragged herself back into the saddle, sodden jeans sticking to soggy leather. The cattle plodded at a maddening pace as Diana squirmed against the sand in her pants. Worse, she caught Brock grinning at her, and she knew he realized her discomfort.

"We're almost there, Diana." He liked the way her

blue T-shirt molded itself to her breasts, but he tried to avoid a direct stare. "You really don't look half-bad. Just hold that elevated nose pose, and nobody'll notice the mud on your pants."

"Maybe not, but they're sure to hear the water squishing in my boots."

"That would shoot the image all to hell, wouldn't it? We'll come up with something."

Once they were near the corrals, the cows followed their customary route through the open gates. Brock signaled to Diana with a tilt of his head, and she trailed after him. He led her away from the activity at the pens, circling around until they arrived at the back door of the house.

"Shower and change in fifteen minutes and then go sauntering out there like you just went in to check on dinner," Brock instructed, taking the reins on the mare after Diana's noticeably wobbly dismount.

Before she could protest that it would take fifteen minutes just to get rid of all the grit, he gave her a cocky wink, then wheeled both horses in the direction of the corrals.

Perversely, Diana took her time in the shower, watching the sand she'd brought into the tub find its way to the drain. Her muscles felt like tapioca pudding, and the sand embedded under her nails attested to the clawing she'd had to do to haul herself out of that nasty little stream. What a ridiculous sight she must have been, dripping and screaming and trying to pull that horse out of the water with her scrawny arms.

Her mind replayed the scene: Brock's arrival, his calm handling of the horse, his hands on her shoulders, the concern in his charcoal-brown eyes, his . . . No, the kisses were the other night. He'd kissed her the other night, and she'd made a fool of herself today.

Diana heard clattering in the kitchen as she was tying her sneakers. "I'm really sorry about the boots, Jackie," she called to her friend.

"Keep your fingers off the cake, and I'll let you lick the bowl," Jackie was heard to promise before she called out, "No problem, Diana. They'll dry."

"Can I help you in the kitchen?" Diana headed down the hall in that direction. "I can probably ride herd on small boys better than I can . . ." There was Brock, leaning against the counter, sucking on one forefinger. "Cows."

"The *small* boys I can handle." Jackie laughed. "It's the big boys who give me a real pain."

"Told you I'd come after you." Brock licked his lips, enjoying whatever his finger had pilfered, but his smiling eyes challenged Diana.

"The best help you could give me would be to keep this big lug out of my frosting," said Jackie.

"All set for the initiation?" Pushing away from the counter, Brock hooked his thumbs into the pockets of his jeans. With his straw cowboy hat pushed back on his head to reveal his dark, curly hair and his decidedly mischievous grin, he looked like a little boy with something devious up his sleeve.

"Do I get thrown in the water trough?" Diana's dubious expression indicated that there were limits to her good sportsmanship.

"You've already been there. No, I'll go easy on you, since you got off to a bad start this morning. Ever give shots?"

He was hopeless. "Certainly. I'm a nurse in my spare

time. I vaccinated the entire U.S. Navy against foot-in-mouth disease back in—''

"Really? Funny I didn't recognize you right off. I never met a nurse I didn't like."

"I'm sure I made an impression on you. Turn around; let me see if it's still there."

With a wicked grin, Brock flicked open his big, silver belt buckle and prepared to turn his back.

"Brock Reed, don't you dare drop your pants in my kitchen!" Jackie shrieked. "Go on outside, you two."

"You'd better keep him away from your cattle, Jackie. His vaccination obviously didn't take."

Brock gestured gallantly for Diana to precede him to the back door. "It's foot-*and*-mouth disease, by the way."

"Not in your case."

Diana found that giving shots was not her forte. Hating needles herself, she balked when she tried to jab the thing into some poor cow's hide. After several abortive attempts with the vaccinating gun, she was relieved of that assignment. She watched while the efficient crew treated the cows for worms, pinkeye, and errant horns. Horns that were found to be growing in a convolution toward the cow's head were sawed off using a thin steel wire. The cattle that Jim had bought recently were vaccinated, while all were given vitamin injections.

Cows and calves were turned into a pen downwind of the rest of the activity. There they were sprayed for flies. Diana was handed a hose attached to a huge tank, and she sprayed while Brock kept the cows moving in a circle so that the spray would reach all sides. He warned her that he did not need to be sprayed for flies himself, and she wished silently that the tank did not contain chemicals. The animals were then turned into a small pen, where they bellowed and bleated, cows searching for their calves, calves anxious for their mothers.

"By the looks of you, I'm not much of an initiator." Brock hooked an arm over the top of the corral rail by Diana's perch.

"How so?"

"You're too clean. Nobody works cows and comes out of it this clean."

"I managed to sneak in a shower and a change of clothes, remember?"

Brock smiled. "Well, you get the sportsmanship award for the day." His hand fell on Diana's shoulder, his arm draped loosely behind her back, and they started toward the house.

The rest of the crowd had long since gathered on the deck. Several wives had shown up, and there was a yard full of children. Brock introduced Diana around as he opened the can of beer that was handed him. Diana greeted all the strange faces, grateful that Brock introduced her as "Jackie's friend from Rhode Island" rather than the "lady lawyer."

Jackie had the picnic buffet set out by the time introductions were over, and Diana watched with some indignation as the men served themselves first. True, they had worked hard, but this seemed a bit crude. The women followed, some working on several plates at once, pausing to trumpet to their young. "Randy, come on and eat now. Bring Mikey. You want beans?"

Jackie stood back and surveyed the scene, watching to see that everyone had what he wanted, pointing out the location of salt, forks, and toothpicks.

"I'm not being much help," Diana said apologetically.

"Nonsense," Jackie retorted. "You helped all morning.

Get something to eat and visit with people. Did you meet everyone?''

"Yes, Brock took care of the introductions." Diana glanced in his direction, noting that his plate was almost empty and that he was engrossed in conversation with two men who seemed to be enjoying her potato salad in great quantities. He sensed her attention and smiled even before he swung his gaze in her direction. Diana caught herself smiling back immediately, pleased when he excused himself in the middle of the conversation and sought her company. And she forgot all about Jackie.

"You haven't eaten anything, have you?" Brock asked.

"Not yet. I was waiting for someone to say 'ladies first,' but nobody did."

"I told you we didn't go in for sex discrimination," he teased. "You women are gonna have to make up your minds whether you want to be ladies or *persons*." He hung a trace of sarcasm on the last word.

"Why can't we be both?"

"Because when I open the door for a lady, she smiles and thanks me, but when I open the door for a *person*, she barks at me. 'What's the matter? Do I look helpless?' And I'm standing there holding the door, looking ridiculous, while she refuses to go in. I never know whether I'm coming or going with women anymore."

"That's quite a straight line, mister, but I think I'll leave it alone. Your ego has obviously suffered enough. If you're going back to the table for seconds, I think I'll join you."

"After you?" he asked.

Diana let him stand there with his hand out for a moment before she took the lead, laughing with him.

*   *   *

Long into the late afternoon the Reinhart yard was filled with activity. As if they hadn't tossed enough loops during the day, the men roped plastic steer heads stuck into bales of hay just for practice. Meanwhile the women cleaned up remnants of the meal, then sat on the deck visiting and reprimanding children when the roughhousing got out of hand. Some of the women, including Diana and Jackie, were coaxed into joining in on a softball game.

After sandwiches and desserts and the last of the beer were served, most of the neighbors gathered their children and headed for home. All except Brock and Christopher.

Brock helped Jim ride through the cows, making sure they were "mothered-up," and then the herd was turned back out to the pasture. Meanwhile, Diana bewailed the soreness in her legs while Jackie bathed her tired children, tossing little Christopher into the tub for good measure. Once they were clean and had gobbled up one more cookie apiece, all three children went quietly to sleep.

Jackie and Diana planted themselves wearily in the porch swing, listening to it creak as they kept it swaying, each with one lazy foot. They giggled over Diana's plunge into the creek.

"Oh, Jackie, what a peaceful, happy place this is. If you could only bottle it and sell it. What a marvelous alternative to Valium."

"I wish you'd thought of it that way sooner. You should've called me long ago."

"What would you have done?" Diana asked.

"I would've gone out there. I would have . . . we could have talked, just like in the old days."

"I was so sure I could handle everything myself. I didn't tell anybody until . . . until I had to get help—professional help. I'm a long way from the wreck I'd become. Now I'm ready to talk. I'm *able* to talk now, and to spend some time with my best friend.'' Diana reached for Jackie's hand and squeezed it, reminding herself again that she could reach out to other people, that she had, indeed, freed herself from seclusion.

"And make new friends?'' Jackie asked.

"Yes, I think I'm ready for new friends.'' The sound of boot heels scraping in the gravel penetrated the silent night, as if on cue. "Brock's a lot of fun. I think I'm even ready for some fun. I can't remember the last time I actually took part in something I really enjoyed.''

The two men walked into the circle of light cast by the big lamppost behind the backyard. Diana and Jackie sat in the dark, watching and waiting. "Brock's very handsome, isn't he?'' Diana mused.

"Mm-hmm. So's Jim.''

"Mm-hmm. They're both a little bow-legged, aren't they? Is that what makes them swagger when they walk?''

"That and the fact that they probably know we're watching.'' Both women burst into girlish giggles.

"You girls waiting up for us?'' Jim hailed as he swung open the picket gate.

"We're enjoying the peace and quiet. All the young-'uns are bathed and sleeping,'' Jackie reported.

"Thanks, Jackie,'' Brock said, then stood for an awkward moment by the swing before he ventured, "What would it take to get you to trade places with me, Jackie? I'll bring you any chair you say.''

"I think we oughta turn in, Jack, don't you?'' Jim suggested. A male conspiracy.

"Okay, Brock, you can have my spot. But remember: This is my best friend here.''

"There's beer in the fridge,'' Jim supplied. Then, with a

hand at the back of his wife's neck, he gave a gentle nudge toward the door. "Come on, Everybody's Mother."

There was quiet. The porchlight went out, and there was night darkness. *Strange,* Diana thought, *this is just as tantalizing as it was fifteen years ago.* She swallowed audibly when Brock lifted his arm and draped it across the back of the swing.

"Well, now I think we're supposed to say a few things about the stars and make out," Brock surmised.

"Do you think Everybody's Mother has gone to bed yet?"

"I have it on good authority that she was headed straight for bed, although it may be a while before she goes to sleep."

"So . . . tell me about the stars. You seem to have more of them here than we do back east."

"Listen, I'm sorry I let you fall into the creek. Didn't sour you on riding, did it?"

"It wasn't your fault. I managed that all on my own—strictly against the wishes of your fine horse."

"You'll let me take you riding again, then?"

"After my muscles recover from today's outing."

There was another moment of cricket voices and a creak of the swing. "I feel like a fool, Diana. I can't think of a single glib line. I think I'm nervous."

"You were pretty smooth the other night."

"I know. Now my palms are sweating. It's been a good day, and I enjoyed spending it with you. And now . . . damn, I feel like a kid."

"It would be simpler if we were kids. There'd be nothing behind us to complicate our feelings—no regrets, no hurts—and we'd be just on the threshold . . ." Her voice trailed off as his arm tightened around her, and he nuzzled her hair, kissing the soft pulse point at her temple. Her stomach contracted, and she lost track of her next words.

"It won't be simple with us," he whispered, and he kissed her again, "but I plan to enjoy more days like today . . . with you." His lips embarked on a slow descent to the side of her neck.

"Do you think you'll be able to overcome your . . . shyness?"

"I'm sure gonna try like hell," he promised, and he covered her mouth with his, taking her hand and putting it behind his neck. He pulled her into his arms, drawing the warm sweetness from her mouth and filling it with the gentle probings of his tongue. His shoulders felt hard beneath her hands, and she stroked the shelf of muscle, reveling in the strength of his embrace. He worked his mouth over hers, his kiss at once tender and demanding. Diana's fingers sank in the cushion of curls at the nape of his neck.

Redefining his claim on her mouth with slower, gentler kisses, Brock caressed her back, learning her slightness, discovering the shape of her spine, her shoulders, her slender waist. His fingers approached the underside of her breast. The slight tremble he felt beneath his hands exhilarated him, and he filled his hand with cotton-covered flesh.

His teasing caress brought a warm rush of flutters to the depths of Diana's stomach. His lips were teasing, too, but she captured them with her own when they hovered within striking range. With an insistent kiss, she told him everything he needed to know. The summer top's strap slipped easily from her shoulder. Her breast lay softly in his hand, his calluses causing shivery sensations as they brushed her smooth skin. His thumb made little circles over her nipple, and she felt her flesh tighten. His name spilled from her mouth at the tail of a moan.

"I just want to touch you, Diana." His voice was like sandpaper, deep in his throat. "Just touch. . . . Oh, God, that's not all I want. . . ." He smothered her mouth with another kiss, plunging his tongue inside, creating an image of what he really wanted.

Both were trembling when his mouth abruptly released hers, and the night seemed to close in around them. Diana closed her eyes, aware that their breathing was a quietly desperate sound. The hand that caressed her dutifully returned the strap of her top to her shoulder, and he pulled her against his chest.

"You're right, Brock," she breathed. "It won't be simple with us."

He smoothed her hair with an unsteady hand, surprised by the hammering in his chest and the dry feeling in his throat. *Now's the time to run, Brock. This is more complicated than you can afford.*

But when he buried his nose in her hair and inhaled that delicious citrus, he knew he wasn't about to run.

He felt too damn good.

Chapter Four

"*I* want to see you today."
The voice on the phone held none of the casual lightness of the recently acquired friend suggesting a get-together for lunch. The serious tone surprised Diana, even startled her.

"You saw me yesterday—last night."

"I want to see you again today. You're not busy?"

"Well, no, Brock. I—"

"We'll be over in a few minutes."

Diana swung the receiver up and clapped it onto the hook. She guessed she had nothing better to do. She *knew* she had nothing better to do. The minute he'd left the night before she'd found herself missing him. It was probably his decisive approach that rankled a bit now. He had a habit of not asking about her willingness to see him. But she was free today, and—she smiled to herself—he'd pushed her adrenaline release with just a phone call. Since she'd met him, she'd noticed an improvement in her mood. Why not enjoy?

Not fifteen minutes had passed when Brock's blue-and-silver pickup roared into the gravel driveway. Christopher tumbled out first, racing for the sandbox where Jeff was busy with a fleet of trucks.

"You're too late for breakfast and too early for lunch," Jackie said, admitting him into her kitchen. "You must be after something besides a free meal."

"Looking for cheap labor. Thought I'd see what I could get out of your houseguest. Think she can feed the stock?"

"It's a good thing you're not looking for kitchen help, Mr. Reed." Both heads turned as Diana walked into the kitchen. "That would have ended our friendship."

"Good morning," he said, offering a smile and enjoying the pleasure of looking at her before adding, "No, you showed some promise yesterday. I think I can make a respectable ranch hand out of you."

"I can't imagine it could be more than a two-lesson course. After today, I'll expect wages."

Brock favored Jackie with a conspiratorial wink. "This lady's too damned cocky, Jackie. An honest day's work is long overdue."

"I gave you an honest day's work yesterday," Diana reminded him. "My agonizing muscles can attest to that."

"Oh, geez, that's right. I'll bet you're pretty sore. I'll keep that in mind. I'll get you back before the cock crows. Don't wait up, Jackie; I've got a long list of chores."

"Chris can stay and play with Jeff," Jackie suggested.

Brock considered a moment before answering. "No, he'd better go home with me. I dumped him off on you once this week already."

"Brock, you know it's no problem. Jeff loves to—"

"Not today, Jackie." Brock's tone bordered on abruptness, but it quickly returned to the characteristically casual as he asked, "Ready, Little Rhodey?"

"I take it this is an invitation to spend the day at your

ranch," Diana said. "You know, you really have yet to
ask me if I want to go."

Brock stared at her for a moment, then frowned slightly.
"I called you a little while ago. I thought I . . . didn't I
ask you to come over to my place?"

Diana shook her head slowly. "You just said you wanted
to see me."

His grin only hinted of mischief. "Pardon me, ma'am. I
guess I got a little ahead of myself. Would you care to be
my guest for lunch?"

Diana smiled, her green eyes bright with delight. "I
would enjoy that very much, Mr. Reed. Thank you."

Two steps brought Brock close enough to grab Diana's
hand and tug her toward the back door. "Let's get a move
on, then. After lunch, we've got work to do. Ever clean
stalls?"

"Not since I helped Hercules with his twelve labors. See
you later, Jackie," Diana called just before the screen
door clicked shut behind her.

Brock's house was older than the Reinharts' and much
bigger. Like an old-timer's story, it tended to ramble—a
big front porch, a second floor with dormers, a saltbox-
style lean-to in the back, and a newer addition on the
south side. They entered through the lean-to, which Brock
called the mud room. Raincoats and jackets hung on wall
hooks, and a rack along one wall held an assortment of
boots. The room held a washer, a dryer, a freezer, and
shelves full of home-canned goods.

"Somebody's been pretty busy in the kitchen," Diana
said, surveying the jars. "Surely not you, though."

"Nope. My mother still can't think of food in small
quantities. I thought once she moved to town and I plowed

her old garden under, she'd stop doing this. But she's still at it—puts summer up in jars.'' He gestured to a pair of steps that led to a landing, which Diana traversed ahead of him to find herself in a big blue-and-white kitchen. It was clean and sunny, very much a mother's kitchen.

"It's such a big house, Brock. Why did your mother move out and leave you and Christopher to ramble around, just the two of you?"

"That was part of the deal. She said there were too many memories here. She wanted to start over, but couldn't bear to let this place pass into a stranger's hands."

Christopher opened the door to a broom closet and pulled out a shoe box, setting it down on the blue linoleum floor.

"Close the closet door, son," Brock reminded him, and as the boy complied, Brock continued, "There are times when I would like having Mom around, especially for Christopher, but I know how this place dredges up old memories. . . . How about some lemonade?"

"Yeah, lemonade!" Christopher chirped as he lined a tiny fleet of cars bumper to bumper on the floor.

"Yeah, lemonade," Diana echoed, gazing at the uncluttered counters, the crisp gingham curtains, and the freshly waxed floor. "This place is pretty spotless for a bachelor pad."

"We do fine on our own, don't we, Chris? Women don't have a corner on being able to keep house and raise kids. I run the vacuum, and Christopher dusts the furniture."

"And Gramma washes the clothes sometimes and waxes the floor so you can't come in for twenty minutes and vacuums *under* the sofa where toys get lost."

"Oh, so you fellas *do* get a little help, hmm? Grandma comes to help out once in a while?"

"About once a week," Brock admitted.

"And she brings cookies," Christopher added.

"I've tried to get her to lay off, but you can't kick your own mother out of the house. She sneaked in here yesterday while I was gone and committed a total cleanup." He handed Diana a tall glass of lemonade.

She smiled. "So you thought today would be a good time for a guest."

"Seemed like a good idea." Brock returned the smile.

"So what's for lunch? Need any help?"

"It's all taken care of," Brock assured her with a wave of his hand.

"Courtesy of Grandma Reed?"

"Best cook in the county."

Brock gave Diana a tour of the house, which had obviously been furnished by a woman of another generation. The Victorian furniture was draped with crocheted doilies and embroidered table runners. A Persian rug graced the polished hardwood floor in the living room.

The newer addition was a large family room, the part of the house that truly seemed lived in. There the plump cushions on the modular seating were dished a little, and there was a TV, a pool table, a stereo, and an overflowing box of toys in the far corner of the room.

"I'll bet this is where you put your Christmas tree," Diana guessed.

"Yeah, this is my room—my furniture, my style. I tried to get my mother to take some of that other stuff out, but she said it belonged here. I guess it does, but I don't know what to do with it. Nobody ever sits in the living room, except my mother."

"It must have been hard for her to move."

"She spends a lot of time here. This is what they

wanted, Diana, their son on the home place. My grandfather built this house. Before that my grandparents lived in a little three-room house down by the creek, near where my great-grandparents lived in a soddy. My roots are here.''

''There aren't many people in this day and age who can look at the ground beneath their feet and say that. Roots must be important to you.''

''What's important is providing a secure home and a good life for my son. I'm glad that I carry on the family tradition in the process.'' At the sound of the back door squeaking open and shut, Brock predicted, ''That'll be Jake, my hired man, which means it's time to eat.''

Jake was a leathery-looking man dressed in red plaid and faded denim—tall, spare, and in his sixties. Ducking out of the little washroom off the kitchen, he seemed a little flustered when Diana followed Brock into the room. A baseball-style cap advertising farm machinery was snatched from his head, leaving a ruffled thatch of graying hair to be smoothed back by the same hand that held the cap.

''Diana Peters, this is Jake Barnes, the man who keeps this place running on course,'' Brock said. ''Diana's here visiting the Reinharts, Jake. She and Jackie were in college together.''

Jake fumbled with the cap momentarily before he thrust a hand in Diana's direction. ''Pleased to meet you, ma'am. Brock didn't tell me we was havin' company.''

''I didn't want you to spend all morning fixing yourself up. The lady's here to see me, not you,'' Brock teased.

''Thought you said she was here to see the Reinharts. Have a seat, ma'am. The boy forgets his manners.'' Jake remembered his, though, pulling a chair back from the kitchen table for Diana.

"Thank you, Mr. Barnes. I thought maybe I could help with—"

"No, ma'am, you're a guest. You got the coffee on, Brock?"

"Not yet." Brock headed for the refrigerator. "C'mon, Chris, you can set the table. Jake wants to play host."

"No, sir, I'm just a hired hand, and this here's part of my wages. You wanna keep good help around, you gotta put three square meals on the table every day. Dollar a day and found—that's the deal."

"You do a little better than that," Brock muttered as he delivered platters of cold fried chicken, coleslaw, and potato salad to the table. "I'll bet you had enough of this kind of stuff yesterday, Diana."

"No, it all looks very good."

"You'll like this potato salad better. Jackie doesn't use enough—I don't know—pickles or something."

"Prepare yourself for a moment of chagrin, Mr. Reed. That was *my* potato salad."

Jake choked back a chortle. "You sure have a way of jackin' your jaw up with your boot heel, boy."

"Funny you should mention that," Diana noted with a coy smile at Brock, who was pulling out a chair for himself. "I was telling Brock just yesterday that he might be due for a foot-in-mouth booster."

"He'll be due for a boot in the butt from me if he don't treat you right, ma'am. You just let me know."

"Hey, in case nobody's noticed, I'm sitting right here,' Brock protested in mock indignation. "You can give me my comeuppance directly. I didn't mean to say your potato salad was *bad*, Diana, but this is better. Here, try it." He plunked a spoonful on her plate, then pointed the spoon in Jake's direction. "And *you,* you old goat, you work for *me,* remember?"

"Only because I feel sorry for ya, boy. You still need somebody around tellin' you how to mind your manners and how to get your cue lined up with the ball."

Diana giggled. "I like this man."

"Tell you what, ma'am, if I was just a few years younger, you'd like me even better, and I'd give the boy here a run for his money."

"Hell, Jake, you were worse lookin' twenty years ago than you are now. At least now you've got some—what do they call it?—character in your face," Brock teased.

"They call 'em wrinkles, boy, and that's what they'll be when you get 'em, too. Mind you, ma'am, the boy ain't dumb. He's real bright, in fact. He's just short on horse sense, which is what I got, an' plenty of it. Yes, sir."

"And how long have you worked here, Mr. Barnes?" Diana asked, smiling.

"Since the boy here was about that size." He nodded toward Christopher. "The boy and me, we kept this place goin' after his dad passed on."

"Jake, how about we change the subject over to your side of the fence. Did you get that south quarter baled up?" Brock asked.

Jake nodded. "Moved on down the line. So damned dry. Might as well knock it down before it all burns up. Second cutting won't be worth much."

"Dry?" Diana asked. "It just rained the other day."

"That was about the only good rain we've had," Brock explained. "After a dry fall and an open winter, we could use about a week's worth. We were lucky, though. Just west of us, they didn't get any."

"Can I ride in the tractor with you today, Jake?" Christopher begged through a mouthful of food.

"Sure, if it's okay with your dad. You plannin' on gettin' any work in today, Brock?"

"Actually, I thought I'd mind my manners and entertain our guest."

"Glad to hear it." Jake turned a relieved look on Diana. "It'd be just like him to drag you over here to get some work out of you."

"Would it?" Diana arched an eyebrow in Brock's direction.

"I should've served you lunch in the dining room and let the help eat by himself in the kitchen," Brock groaned.

"I wouldn't have missed the pleasure of Mr. Barnes's company for the world. You might as well tell us what chores you have planned for me for after lunch, Brock."

"Well, since Jake's determined to spread the manure, maybe you'd like to throw a little slop to the male chauvinist pigs."

"Do they like potato salad?"

"Long as it's got plenty of pickles in it."

"*Believe* me, this does," she said, throwing a wink at Jake.

Jake packed Christopher off in an old red pickup while Diana helped Brock clean up the dishes. "Jake's a lot more than a hired man, isn't he?" she said as she watched the truck churn up a cloud of dust on the gravel road.

"An impossible old goat is what he is," Brock said, chuckling. Then he added, "He's always been like a father to me, even while my old man was still alive. When I played ball in high school, it was Jake who came to the games. My father figured time spent playing was time you could be working.''

''Is Jake a good worker?''

''Hell of a good worker, and he enjoys it. You can work alongside Jake and be talking and laughing, and you're done before you know it. And speaking of work, why don't I show you how to drive a tractor? I think we could make beautiful windrows together, don't you?''

Diana turned to hand him the last of the plates scraped for the dishwasher and offered him a smile on the side. Setting the plate back on the counter, Brock took the smile lightly between his lips and gave it a soft kiss. ''What do you think?'' he asked before she opened her eyes.

''Mmm, I think you serve great dessert here.''

''You like it? Exclusive house recipe. Have another.'' He turned her into his arms and let his mouth close over hers, pulling her up on her toes and into the buoyancy of his kiss. One hand against her shoulder blades eased her to his chest while the other moved just below her waist to hold her close. Then he trailed his mouth from her lips to the side of her neck, which he nuzzled gently.

''You mentioned something about a windrow?'' Diana said breathlessly. ''What's a windrow?''

''That's what you have to do . . .'' A nibble at her ear. ''To get everything lined up . . . um . . . just right . . .'' A nip at the collarbone. ''And all ready. . . .''

''Mmm. Ready for what?''

''For the baler.'' A soft, quiet kiss on her lips. ''We're making hay.''

''While the sun shines?'' Diana opened her eyes and gave him a lazy smile.

''Right. Unless you want more dessert.''

She caught her lower lip in her teeth as though considering. "I try not to overindulge in such rich confections. Especially when I have chores to do."

"Well, there's always supper, with plenty of time afterward for a long, lingering dessert."

The couple piled into Brock's pickup and followed the gravel road for about a quarter of a mile before they turned onto a rutted dirt road. To their left was a purple-and-yellow field, the blooms waving in the breeze like a grass sea awash with colored marbles.

"What are those flowers?" Diana asked.

"Alfalfa and sweet clover. That's what we're going to cut."

"What a shame. You want it to look like that?" She pointed to the right, where the grass had been harvested, leaving a cut-pile carpet of yellow-green.

"I want it to look like that," he said, pointing to a big, round quarter-ton bale of hay.

Diana looked at the bales scattered over the field like huge parcels that had escaped the back of a truck. Then one near the road caught her eye, and she gasped. "Oh, my God, what . . . Brock!"

Protruding from the middle of one end of the bale were two legs wearing jeans and a pair of cowboy boots. Brock slowed the pickup beside the ghastly sight, and Diana knew, when she saw the barely suppressed glee in his eyes, that she'd been had.

"Looks like old Jake baled out," Brock said, the chuckle sputtering in his throat.

"Oh, God, I don't believe it!" Diana shrieked. "It looks so real! It looks like somebody's stuck in that bale."

"At Jake's age, that's taking a roll in the hay." Brock laughed.

Diana groaned. "Well, you did it. You had me going with that one."

"I had nothing to do with it. You can thank your champion, Mr. Barnes. He's a lot harder on city slickers than yours truly."

Diana was shaking her head, still laughing at herself, when the pickup nosed over a hill and gave her a view of a windrowed hay field. A corduroy fabric of tan and gold, the ridges of hay piled in straight rows and dried by the sun stood ready for the baler. Brock pointed to the horizon, where a big green tractor seemed to gobble a trail of hay, leaving behind only a huge round bundle.

"There they are," Brock said. "Jake's telling Christopher the same stories he used to tell me—his Pecos Bill rodeo stories, his 'back in the navy' stories. Best bull-throwing artist you've ever heard."

"Does he live with you?"

"He lives in the trailer behind the corrals on the other side of the barn. I offered him a room at the house after the folks left, but he likes having a place of his own, I guess."

"It's lucky for you that he's so good with Christopher. That must take some of the burden off you."

Brock's face seemed to harden. "My son isn't a burden. I don't need help looking after him."

"I just meant that it's nice that . . . that you and Christopher both regard Jake as part of the family. It seems it would make things easier—"

"Chris tags along with Jake sometimes, but I don't use Jake as a baby-sitter. I don't want anyone getting the idea that I'm dumping my kid off on my hired man."

"Who is *anyone*?" Diana asked, studying Brock's reaction with interest.

"Anyone?"

"Who is this *anyone* you're so concerned about?"

Brock sighed, and his eyes apologized for his abruptness. "It isn't you. I guess I'm a little touchy about people's attitudes toward single parents—*male* single parents. Because I'm a man, my suitability is suspect. People are always saying how sad it is for a little guy like that not to have a mother. It's like you said the other night: If Lori decided she wanted him, I'd probably have a fight on my hands."

"Maybe I'll get my sex discrimination case out here yet," Diana said, smiling.

"Representing the reverse side of the coin?"

"Representing the right side. After three years, Christopher belongs with you."

"Yeah, but I can just see her coming up with some amnesia or nervous-breakdown story." Brock shrugged, turning the pickup onto the field and heading toward another green tractor.

"You watch too many movies. Is *this* the tractor I'm supposed to drive?"

"With a little help from your friend. It's very simple— one easy lesson. It's not really a tractor; it's a windrower."

This tractor had a long platform attached to it, and inside the glass-enclosed cab it looked as though the seat were facing backward. Diana watched Brock climb the three little steps that hung near the huge black tire. There was only one seat in there, and Brock sat on it, pushed the straw cowboy hat back on his head, and motioned for Diana to follow.

"Where am I supposed to sit?" she asked, ducking her head inside the door. Brock grinned and pushed the seat back, patting his thigh. "Won't that make it a little difficult to use the accelerator or—God help us—the brake?''

''It has hand controls.'' He laid one hand on an orange knob that looked like part of a gearshift. ''This is the throttle. Those foot pedals are for adjusting the platform. Come on in and get comfortable. I'll turn on the air-conditioning.''

''And I always thought farming was such hard work,'' Diana mumbled, hoisting herself into the cab. She settled her blue jeans against Brock's, her thighs straddling his, and she reached for the steering wheel. ''You say your hands will be busy with the controls?''

''Pretty much.'' He chuckled, reaching around her to start the motor, flip the switch for the air-conditioning, and put the machine in gear. His chin was perched over her shoulder, and she felt his breath, then a little nibble on her neck. ''You won't have to worry about my hands.'' She started to shoo him away with her hand, but he caught her wrist and put the hand back where it was. ''First rule: Keep your hands on the wheel at all times. Watch the platform.''

Diana felt his thighs flex beneath her and saw the big platform in front of them move, lifting, then settling close to the ground. Then the big green monster was in motion, edging forward. Diana's eyes widened, and she gripped the steering wheel.

''Relax, now. I've got it,'' Brock assured her, planting his left hand just below hers. ''First we'll sort of draw an outline around the field, so we know where to end each row.''

The machine moved slowly, the cutter bar in front chomping down everything in its path. Dust and bits of grass danced in a little cloud over the length of the platform. When they had gone some distance, Brock lifted the platform, turned the entire machine at a right angle, and moved out again. Once he had marked off his field, he let Diana do most of the steering.

Bouncing along on his lap, she felt a surge of power, sitting high over the big grass mower and watching it knock down the field. When she turned to look back at the ridge of grass left in their wake, she caught Brock's smile reflected in his deep brown eyes. "Watch where you're going, lady. You're liable to run into a tree."

"There isn't a tree in sight."

"A fence post, then."

Up and down the field they went, weaving another patch of corduroy. After more than an hour, they walked back to the pickup and shared the iced tea Brock had brought in a Thermos.

"Had enough of this farming, Diana? I can take you back if you like," Brock offered.

"Am I getting too heavy for you?"

"You kidding? This is the most fun I've ever had knocking down hay. But I don't want to ruin a good thing."

"Hmm," she considered, surveying the field. "If we finish this field, would you consider that to be an honest day's work?"

"Well, it's honest work, but not worth a whole day's wages. We'll still have stock to feed and a busted gate to fix."

"Can't quit now, then, can we? If your lap can hold out, then I guess my bottom can."

"My lap's very content with this arrangement," Brock assured her, draping an arm over her shoulder as they started the walk back to the windrower.

It was late afternoon when the field lay cut and the

windrower was left near the dirt road. Brock explained that they'd have to walk back to the pickup because driving the windrower would mean messing up their work.

"Next time let's leave the pickup truck where we plan to end up. Then we'll have the walk at the beginning rather than at the end," Diana suggested, wiping the back of her wrist across her forehead.

"Next time?"

"I'm here to get a taste of the country life—good, clean living, *hard* work. Since you've already discerned that the novelty appeals to me, I'm sure you're more than ready to take advantage of my willing nature. You figure you'll get all your haying done before I leave," Diana said with a knowing smile.

"You have great insight."

"So I've been told. In fact, I had an English teacher once who—"

"You also have tremendous hindsight. Next time the pickup goes at the end of the field."

As they drove over a little rise, leaving the hay field behind, Diana turned on her seat to look back at her work. "They're a little crooked in spots, aren't they?" There was a note of disappointment in her voice.

Brock slowed to a stop, hooked his arm over the seat, and looked in the same direction. "I wouldn't call them crooked. I'd say they're . . . contoured. Damn good for the first time out."

"I take that to be a genu-ine compliment, and I thank you kindly," Diana drawled.

Through the kitchen window, Diana watched Christopher jump from the pickup seat into Jake's waiting arms. But for his sneakers, the boy was a miniature version of his father—a wavy crop of near black hair that was due for a trim, hot-fudge-sundae eyes, and a ready smile. Robbie would have been almost three, walking and talking, becoming a little person just like this.

"They back?" Brock asked, entering the kitchen.

"What? Oh, yes, they're coming in now. How does this look?" She gestured toward the salad bowl. "I put spinach in it. Surprising to find fresh spinach in a bachelor's refrigerator."

"I told you: my mother was here yesterday. And that's just the way I like it. The grill's ready." He snatched a cherry tomato from the bowl and popped it in his mouth before moving to the refrigerator for the steaks. "Most of that stuff is out of her garden. How do you like your steak?"

"Rare. How do you like your coffee?"

"Strong. You sure think you have bachelors pegged," he mused on his way to the door. Then she heard him tell Jake and Christopher to wash for supper.

"Evenin', ma'am," Jake greeted her. "See that boy's still got you workin'."

Diana nodded. "Did you see those windrows I made? Weren't they great?"

"Yes, ma'am, they sure were." Jake ushered Christopher into the bathroom and pushed the little stepstool up to the sink. Turning on the water, Jake asked, "How'd you like my bales?"

"You really should be more careful, Mr. Barnes. You never know who might be sleeping in your field. Just today we found one poor fellow rolled up in the middle of a bale, and Brock says that's the third one this week. Scared the life out of me."

"It wasn't real," Christopher assured her earnestly. He

glanced at Jake, who gave him a conspiratorial wink. "It was just a joke—to make you laugh."

Diana smiled at the boy. "You did make me laugh, Christopher. It was a very funny joke. And I was just kidding about the man."

"Don't want you to run away again," Christopher said. Then he told Jake, "She scares easy."

"She laughs easy, too, though. That's the best kind of woman, button. Remember that."

Diana had never tasted better steak, and both men assured her that North Dakota beef was the best in the world. Brock had roasted corn on the cob on the grill, and Diana had turned a loaf of French bread into garlic toast.

"Actually," Diana said, "I haven't eaten a whole lot of beef lately. I hear you ranchers have been injecting your cattle with hormones or something. I get my ration of cancer-causing agents in diet soda."

"And in that air you breathe out there on the East Coast," Brock judged.

"Is it true? Are you guys slipping something strange into America's all-beef patties?"

"I don't know about 'the guys,' but this is my beef, and I didn't put in anything stranger than grass and corn. You're the one who's doing something strange. How can you smother a good piece of beef in steak sauce like that?"

"Mmm, I love it." Diana grinned.

Diana shared the cleanup chores with the men. They pitched in together as though they'd always been a team in the kitchen. After Christopher had been tucked into bed, Jake stayed in the family room to watch the end of a movie on TV. Outside, Diana helped Brock pour sweet-smelling grain into the horses' feed bunks. It was a hot night, and it felt good to be out of the house.

She watched a colt follow its mother to the sound of the grain and greedily latch on to the mare's teat when she lowered her head and nuzzled the grain. How did it feel to nurse a baby? You should have tried it when you had the chance, Diana told herself. It might have made a difference. The colt was certainly healthy looking.

"Want to auction off your thoughts?" Brock asked. "I'll start the bidding at a penny."

"I was just thinking about horses and hay and windrows— 'country matters,' as Shakespeare would say."

"As I remember, 'country matters' in Shakespeare's plays meant something more interesting." Brock tossed his grain bucket over the fence before draping both forearms over Diana's shoulders.

"Yes," Diana mused, "I think Hamlet suggested lying in Ophelia's lap, and she—"

"She got all embarrassed, and he said he meant to lay his *head* in her lap. He was a real rascal. I played the part in a high school production." Brock smiled, throwing a nod in the direction of an irregular pyramid of square bales standing outside the corral. "How would you like to see the view from the haystack?"

" 'You are merry, my lord,' " Diana quoted, one brow arched in coy protest.

"Yes, I am, but I really want to show you the view. 'Do you think I meant country matters?' "

"I think Ophelia got herself drowned for all her troubles, and I decided yesterday that is not the way I want to go."

"Ah, yes, excellent hindsight." He squeezed her hand. "I just want to show you a bird's-eye view of my little principality. I promise not to bore you with a trumped-up play." He led her through the gate.

"Nor fool's play?"

"Nor foul play, but it *is* playtime."

"And you certainly are playful." Diana laughed as she looked up at the twenty-foot stack. "How do we scale this part of your *play*ground?"

"Child's play, my dear," Brock quipped with a flourish. "Just climb the step."

"Are there mice in here?" she asked, ascending the stack one bale at a time.

Brock was enjoying the pleasure of bringing up the rear. "Mice? Oh, just field mice, but they're out *play*ing the field."

"Groan." She reached the top of the stack. "Ta-daa! I claim this mountain for the queen and the Motherland." She took a sweeping bow and sat down.

"You would." Brock plopped down beside her. "So much for my principality."

"Mmm, it's cooler up here." She swept the hair off the back of her neck and caught the night breeze on her face. "I love the view." Two windows in the house were illuminated, and the light in the corral still burned. She listened to the sound of horses crunching oats and smelled the hay. "And I *have* enjoyed this day."

"You're a good sport, Diana."

"That's an interesting compliment," she said, glancing at him curiously. "One that I don't think I've been paid before."

"You're fun to be with on an ordinary day, just doing ordinary things, and you take everything in graceful stride."

He caught a wisp of hair and lifted it away from her

face. "Your activities aren't exactly ordinary fare for me," she said.

"Am I ordinary fare for you?" He tucked her hair behind her ear as he spoke.

"Not at all," she admitted, closing her eyes when she felt the small strokes of his lower lip against her temple. "You are . . . very rare North Dakota steak." He was nibbling her ear now, his breath warm.

"With lots of sauce?" he asked.

"Mmm." Her mouth was open for his kiss, for the taste of his tongue as he caressed her neck with shy fingertips. Involuntarily her hands reached for his waist as she tried to draw a steadying breath. "Heights make me dizzy."

"Heights have nothing to do with it." He cupped his hands over her shoulders and lowered her to the prickly hay as he covered her mouth with his. He thrust his tongue into the warmth of her mouth and stroked her, savored her, stirred her deep inside. Excitement crackled between them. Impatiently he pulled her shirt loose from her jeans and slipped his hand inside.

His was the touch of pure wool, slightly abrasive but gentle and warm. His work-roughened fingers used her ribs as stairsteps, negotiating them one at a time. When he reached her bra, he read the pattern of the lace as if it were braille, and he put a kiss into the pocket above her collarbone. Her breast settled in the palm of his hand, and he dipped his fingers into the cup. Her flesh expanded, and his fingers were blissfully trapped.

He slipped the strap over her shoulder, kissed her mouth, and made her nipple hard and round against the ball of his thumb. He wanted to love them as they deserved to be loved, but he groaned and flattened his hand against her, dragging his mouth from hers and burying his nose in the hair at the nape of her neck.

Diana turned her face toward his, and her lips met his cheekbone and kissed him there. "I guess we both know how awkward this is," she whispered.

"I want you in my bed, Diana."

"Well, unless your name is Little Boy Blue, I'd guess this isn't it."

Brock's breath was released in a chuckle, and he put the bra strap back where he'd found it. "Very effective. I take it you find my haystack less than comfortable."

"I thought haystacks were supposed to be fluffy piles of soft, yellow stuff."

Brock raised his head and grinned down at her. "Yeah, since the invention of the baler, rolling in the hay ain't what it used to be."

"Ouch!" Diana squealed, squirming. "Something bit me!"

"I can't imagine what would *dare* to bite you."

"A field mouse, maybe?"

The chuckle came from deep in Brock's throat. "Or a hayrack rat." He pulled her against him, pressing her head to his shoulder. "Stay close. I'll fight them off."

But no attack came, and Brock was glad because he didn't feel like fighting. He felt like cuddling, and Diana was a good partner for it.

Suddenly the horizon lit up, and Diana propped herself on her elbows. "What was that?"

"Heat lightning." He sat up with a sigh. "Which means we'd better get down from here before it curls our hair."

It happened again—jagged white etchings snaking silently across the horizon. Brock slid off the top layer of bales and offered Diana a hand. She was transfixed. "I didn't hear any thunder."

"It's heat lightning," he repeated as he coaxed her down. "Sneaks up on you without a sound." He gave her a quick, hard, highly charged kiss. "But it's dangerous."

"Electrifying," she whispered.

Chapter Five

The decision to drive out here hadn't been made during one of her saner moments. Looking past the ruffled yellow swag in the kitchen at the domestic backyard scene, Diana wondered what had led her to suppose that imposing on this family would deliver her from the sterility of her life. Moments before, she'd been sitting with Jackie and Jim and the children at the picnic table, and she'd laughed with them, enjoying the summer supper outside.

The feeling had hit her all at once—that backsliding sensation that made everything around her look one-dimensional and distant, that made her feel as though she'd just been pressure-sealed inside a jar. Suddenly she found herself looking through the glass at a scene she had no real part in. She'd excused herself from the table.

When the phone rang she flinched. She didn't want to answer it, didn't want to talk to anyone just now; but she dreaded the grating sound of a second ring.

"This is the Reinhart residence," Diana answered crisply.

"Reinhart residence, huh? Is this their secretary?"

"No, I'm a houseguest. With whom do you wish to speak?"

"The houseguest will do nicely. You alone?"

"No, I . . . Brock?"

"Yes, Brock. I could've sworn I'd made more of an impression on you."

The voice released the pressure inside the jar. "I . . . yes, you . . . I'm sorry, Brock. I was just . . . outside."

"If you're not real busy, I thought maybe we'd drop over . . . or you could come over here."

Diana glanced back out the window and watched Jackie serve Jeff his third piece of corn. "Why?" she asked distractedly.

"Why? Because I'd like to see you."

"Well, I'm sure you're welcome to visit as you please. I mean, I'm sure—"

"Is something wrong?"

"No . . . nothing."

"I'm *asking* this time. Would you like to—"

"Shall I check with Jackie? I don't think they've made any plans."

"It's *you* I want to see. Is it okay?"

"Yes, I'm free this evening . . . quite free."

Diana slid the receiver back to the cradle, thinking of the irony of her freedom. She was and was not free of her marriage. There were no emotional attachments, but there were such loose ends. They had sold everything—house, furniture, cars. It was the civilized thing to do: sell everything, split the money, start fresh. She'd never lived in an apartment before and had chosen it for its charm, its very Newport character. But there was no picnic table, no backyard.

This was what happened when she let herself dwell on

it. The loose ends were all in her head. How she despised her newfound weaknesses.

"Is something wrong, Diana?"

Diana jumped away from the window at the sound of Jackie's voice as though she'd been caught spying. "No . . . nothing's wrong. Brock just called. He's coming over, and I'm not sure I can handle it tonight."

Setting a salad bowl on the counter, Jackie moved to touch Diana in a way that was solely and reassuringly Jackie. "Can't handle what? Is he . . . coming on too strong?"

"No, it's nothing like that." Diana sighed. "I like Brock very much. He's interesting. Very attractive. I like his . . . I like him very much."

"You said that. So what's to handle?"

Diana slammed the heels of her hands on the counter. "I'm fifteen hundred miles from home, and in a week or two I'm going back to . . . to what's there—my apartment, my office. If I'd wanted an interim fling, I'd have taken a Caribbean cruise. I came here to give my idiotic emotions a rest, Jackie."

"If you don't want to see him, all you have to do is say no."

"But I *do* want to see him. I want what I've always wanted—to be able to guarantee all the outcomes. I want to be in charge of my life and still be able to let myself go. But it doesn't seem to work that way."

The sound of the pickup pulling into the driveway, gravel popping under its tires, caused the women to glance at one another. "If it won't work that way, maybe it's time to try another way," Jackie suggested.

"I don't know any other way."

"Should I tell him you can't *handle* him tonight?"

Jackie's eyes sparkled, but she swallowed the smile. "Don't you dare."

Jackie swept her arm in an after-you gesture, and Diana led the way to the backyard. Brock stood by the picnic table, one boot resting on the bench, conversing with Jim. The children had already found the sandbox.

At Diana's approach, Brock lowered his foot to the ground, straightened up, and offered a warm, handsome smile. Diana knew she'd had a problem moments before, but somehow it must have been left in the house.

Although repeatedly instructed to visit with the men, Diana insisted upon helping Jackie take the remains of supper back in the house while Jim served coffee. That done, the foursome waited out some awkward moments over coffee at the picnic table, no one missing the electric glances between Brock and Diana. At last Brock suggested that he and Diana go for a ride.

"You two go ahead," Jackie encouraged. "And don't worry about Christopher. If you'd let me tell the kids he can spend the night and go with us to the county fair tomorrow, I'd make a big hit with the sandbox contingent."

Brock grinned. "Three cheers for Everybody's Mother! I'll pay you back with an afternoon of cartoons on the video next week."

Bumping along the gravel road, Diana chided herself mentally for her adolescent anxieties. She was alone with an attractive man, headed in the direction of his house, and she wondered what exactly was on his mind for the evening. It had been a long time since she'd played the dating game, and she was a bit rusty. Nowadays, of course, she was supposed to have some objectives of her own, but she rejected everything that came to mind as totally impractical, under the circumstances.

"Why were you so distant when you answered the phone, Diana?"

"What? Oh . . . I was . . . I didn't recognize your voice right away."

"Shall we go to my place? I've got a bottle of wine and a good collection of tapes."

"Country music?" she asked absently.

"City music, too. Whatever suits your mood. And that's cloudy, isn't it? Your mood."

"The weather here seems to be subject to quick changes—sunny one day, cloudy the next. Lately, my moods have been like that. I used to be more . . . consistent."

"Consistently sunny or consistently cloudy?"

"Middle of the road. Consistently dependable. Pleasant."

"As any good businesswoman should be. Only we're not doing business, Diana. We don't have to sit around making faces at each other. No pretty masks, okay? I've had about all the pretty masks I can stand. Let's just go in and talk. You be your cloudy self, or your sunny self . . . whatever. I'll find the right music for your mood."

Left in the family room to make herself comfortable, Diana examined an array of photographs, small ones set on shelves and larger ones on the wall. In particular there were pictures of Christopher at every stage throughout his five years and a series of "young Brock" photos—Brock in a football uniform, Brock wearing a mortarboard and a cocky smile, and a short-shorn Brock in sparkling sailor white.

"What do you think? Did I look pretty good in my uniform?" Brock asked as he came in with two glasses of chilled Chablis.

"You look like girl-in-every-port material. Real Gene Kelly charm here," Diana noted before she set the picture back in its place on the shelf.

Brock handed her a glass with the accompanying flourish of the first several bars of "Anchors Aweigh."

"Is this the mood music I was promised?" Diana asked, offering a salute with the glass.

"I'll go on if you'll do a little soft-shoe." He watched her lashes lower as she sipped. "No? What's your pleasure, then? Violins? I'm a good listener."

"I've done violins to the tune of sixty dollars an hour."

Brock peered into a cabinet, which indeed held an impressive collection of tapes. "Call it fiddle music, and it goes down cheaper. And if we use a steel guitar and a bass, hang up the 'Doctor Is In' sign right below one that spells Budweiser one letter at a time, then the session is free. I just pour the booze and shine the glasses." He selected a tape. "How about James Taylor?"

"Mmm, I like him." Diana sat in a cozy-looking nook on the big, modular couch and sloughed off her sandals, baring her feet and flexing her toes in the thick softness of an area rug.

"Talk to me, Diana." Brock sat next to her, resting his arm along the back of the couch without touching her.

"Am I allowed to put my feet up on the couch?"

" 'Long as they're not muddy. You're also allowed to relax," he said, watching her forefinger trace an immaculate crease down the middle of her thigh.

Diana sipped at her wine again and then tossed her head back as though to give the swallow an extra bit of momentum. "Oh, Brock, this is ridiculous. I find you very attractive."

"Ridiculous? What, have I grown an extra head or something?"

"No, no—*you're* not ridiculous. I am. I came out here with the idea that this would be a very uncomplicated place to be for a while. You know—midwestern, pastoral. Reassurance from Jackie every hour. Nothing more stimulating than sunbathing and late-night reminiscences between two old friends." She looked him in the eye. "I hadn't counted on meeting you."

"Am I a wrinkle in your plans?"

"You're sort of . . . an added dimension."

"You know, Diana," Brock began, his eyes and his fingertips attracted to the embroidery along the shoulder of her pale green blouse, "I'm not one to go out looking for complicated situations for myself, either. I've told myself just to take this one day at a time, and I seem to wake up each day with the same thought on my mind—calling you, seeing you. Do you know what I mean?"

"Yes." She sighed. "I know what you mean."

"What d'ya say we try not to worry about it too much? Why worry about good vibrations?"

"Is that what I'm feeling? Good vibrations?"

"We liked each other right off. That in itself is worth all my spare time for the duration." His voice was quiet, the timbre low, and his mouth was inches from her ear.

"Duration of what?" She inhaled a whiff of woodsy after-shave and concentrated on maintaining the flow of the conversation.

"Of your R and R." Curling his arm around her shoulders, Brock sipped from his glass and watched Diana follow suit. "How often do you get out this way for our restorative rural air?"

"About once every thirty years."

"That often? I guess we'll save the Garden Club tour for the next time around."

Their talk drifted from North Dakota to Rhode Island to an aircraft carrier out at sea. They drank wine and listened to Bob Seger and Willie Nelson, and when Brock suggested dancing in the dim lamplight, it seemed the perfect time and place.

The way he held her was perfect, too, as was the way he touched her with the length of his body, moving with the music, slowly, easily. The palm of his hand against the middle of her back stirred sensuously in time with the gentle, rhythmic sway of their bodies. She wanted him to kiss her, and when she lifted her mouth to him, he granted her wish intuitively. And with his kiss he told her what he wanted of her.

She flowed against his liquid lead, the soft music drifting somewhere behind the sound of his breathing. His tongue played a teasing scale on her neck before returning to assure itself that the best tune could be played on her lips. Her kiss reached for something inside him, something more than good moves and clever words—something of himself saved all these years just for her. She burrowed the fingers of her left hand in the thick hair on the back of his head and pushed herself up on bare toes to offer his mouth every millimeter of her own.

Only their tongues danced now, like two cobras coaxed from a basket, intertwining hypnotically for a song. Brock pulled Diana tightly to him, and she moaned softly when he released her mouth and brushed his lips over her eyelids.

"Let me give you what you want, Diana."

"You . . . don't know . . . what I want." The fluttering of her pulse interfered with her attempt to sound in control. "And there isn't time. . . ." She felt the cushion of his palm at the side of her neck, his thumb lifting her jaw. When she looked at him, his eyes seared through her defenses.

"You want to be close to me . . . and God knows I

can't get close enough to you. There's all the time we want to give each other. All the time these feelings deserve.''

"I'm afraid of feeling, Brock.''

It was there in her eyes as surely as a shadow. She *was* afraid, and it touched him deeply. It was a look he'd never seen in a woman's eyes before. He put his hand around her shoulders to tip her head against his chest. "Believe it or not, I'm a gentleman," he assured her.

"Gentlemen don't impress me. It's a *gentle man* I need. A truly gentle man.''

"Then stay with me tonight," he whispered. "For you, I think I can be that man. Let me try.''

She turned her nose into his shirtfront and inhaled the faintly woodsy scent that mingled with the heady musk of his skin. "I want to stay with you," she said a small voice that she recognized as her own, "just to have you kiss me again.''

Brock rocked her back in his arms and grinned at her. "I do some pretty good kissing, huh?''

"Quite above average.''

"How many more would it take to turn your knees to jelly?''

"I've no idea." She gave him a coy smile. "I'm made of stern stuff. I just thought . . . if there were more kisses in store . . . I'd stick around.''

"Yeah, well . . . I've got this problem of logistics.''

The little kisses he was feathering over her face were making it exquisitely difficult for her to concentrate. "Hmmm? What sort of problem . . . is that?''

"I'd like to take you into the bedroom about now, and I know I'm supposed to sweep you into my arms and carry you in there.''

"But?''

"But I have a feeling you're a woman who goes under her own steam or not at all."

"And you don't think you could haul me up all those steps, anyway." Her eyebrows arched with the challenge, and he swept her off the floor immediately. "Is the master afraid of the stairs?"

"The master is afraid his underwear might be lying on the floor." At the foot of the stairs he quirked a smile, shifting her a little in his arms. "Should I take them two at a time? I suppose it would be bad form to yell 'Charge.' "

"I would say so."

Being cradled against Brock's chest gave Diana a strangely dependent feeling. If he let her go, she would fall. A precarious situation. But it was surprisingly luxurious to let him carry her.

"*This* is my room. Christopher's is right across the hall."

He set her down just inside the door. It was a big room with massive oak furniture and tall windows, which let evening bathe the walls in dim light and shadow. Brock reached for the lamp, then thought better of it. Despite her bravado, he sensed that the wrong move could frighten her, send her scurrying away. He heard her take a deep breath before she moved toward the dresser, watched her touch the bristles of his hairbrush as though testing the quills. She wasn't really sure.

"I like the smell of this cologne . . . on you," she said quietly, fingering the cap on the bottle. How long had it been since she'd seen masculine things arranged on a dresser?

"Thank you."

She passed an old wooden chair, which had a shirt draped over the arm, and stood in front of the open window. From there she could see the gravel road, the fenced patches of field, and the square-topped hills etched against a violet sky. "It's been a long time for me, Brock. I mean, my husband was the last, and I don't usually . . ."

"I think I knew that." He moved silently on the carpet, coming up behind her to place his hands on her shoulders. "You're a special lady, and I want you with me tonight. I want to make love with you, but if you tell me that's not right for you . . . well, then we'll just—"

"You promised me more kisses," she whispered.

"So I did." He turned her toward him. "So I did."

Their lips opened against one another in soft coupling. His tongue stroked the oval of her mouth, and hers replied in kind. Pressing the heels of his hands on either side of her spine, he kneaded the flesh of her back, easing whatever tension she'd built there in a slow trek toward her shoulders. She leaned into his kiss now, and he drew her against him.

His lips trailed softly to the side of her neck, and she shivered. When his hand came up to work the buttons between her breasts, Diana ordered her own hands to stay where they were behind his back. She wanted this moment with this man, and she willed herself not to think beyond it. He released the hook on her bra and the zipper on her slacks, and she felt the cool breeze from the window on her bare back.

The sensation contrasted with the warmth Brock applied to her breasts with his hands. His thumbs teased her nipples to exquisite tightness, and she gasped. "This is where you need to be kissed," he whispered, and he took each nipple in its turn into his tongue. When she swayed toward him, he caught her in his arms and took her to his bed.

She watched him undress as he stood beside the bed. She watched the shadows fall across his face when he leaned down to pull boots and socks from his feet. When he returned to her, he was as naked as she. He dipped his head to her midriff to bisect her torso with a column of feather-light kisses. His tongue drew a dewline across her abdomen, his hands molding her hips like clay.

He moved over her like a hot whirlpool, and something inside her belly yielded in response, all knots of hesitation smoothed into smiling acceptance. Diana whispered his name, and he answered, "I'm here."

Another succulent kiss was delivered to her mouth as he slid his hand between her thighs and gave her such gentle stroking that she soon felt her breath catch in her throat and her body begin to quake.

"You're ready for me now," he murmured near her ear. "Let's make that happen again, sweetheart. I want to go with you this time."

His body seemed to fill hers, yet she arched against him for more. They taxied on an undulating ribbon of runway, gathering momentum—sleek, streamlined, a motion that brooked no resistance to the wind as they were lifted, lifted in the long climb, wingtip to wingtip, wind rolling underneath. Heady and wild and freer than she'd ever felt before, Diana cried out when he raised himself over her on stout arms and poured himself into her. A moment of pounding, surging energy shuddered through her before her senses vaporized and she drifted back to the bedroom on a warm air current of contentment.

Rolling to her side, Brock caught her against him and held her close, letting their hearts have this moment to flutter after one another, two butterflies in the grass. She had let him do all the touching, but Diana now needed to touch him, to wonder over the body that had given her such pleasure. She traced the line of his lowest rib and then smoothed the skin over his abdomen with a delicate hand.

"Mmm, I like that," he murmured after absorbing her touch for several moments. "It's what I need, too, you know . . . to be touched by a truly gentle woman."

Snug against his chest, Diana kissed the nipple there, then smiled. "You may have found something new in me tonight. I feel . . . different."

"Does different mean better or worse?"

"Are you asking me how you . . . measure up?"

"No, I'm asking you how you feel now in comparison with how you felt before we made love. Better or worse?"

"Better. Infinitely better," she said with conviction. "And I don't remember ever feeling this particular kind of better before. It's never been . . . lovemaking hasn't been . . . hasn't ever solved anything for me."

"You told me you were afraid of feeling, and now you tell me you feel good. I'd say we made a little emotional progress there."

"And what about you, Brock? How do you feel?"

"I gave you everything I felt . . . tenderness and . . . real desire for a change, not just . . . I feel good, too, Diana."

"You know what else I feel?" She allowed a pause. "I feel soft. You've made me feel soft, and I like the feeling."

Brock chuckled, running a hand along her back to her bottom. "These callused hands have probably buffed you to a burning pink. I'm sorry, hon. I'm a working man."

"They're wonderful hands," she said, reaching back to cover his hand with hers. "A gentle man's gentle hands."

"Rough enough to make a princess's soft body black

and blue all over. We'll see if you're a *real* princess.''

"Only if you have a pea under the mattress, in which case I shall be sore tomorrow.''

"I'll have proof, girl," he growled, nuzzling her hair. "Which is why I agreed to put you up for the night.''

"You're sure it won't put you out. . . .''

"As long as you don't *put me down,* dear lady, I'll be the perfect host.''

"Promise you won't *put me through* any more word games," she groaned. "Just promise me that, and I'll kiss any toad you say. Even you.''

"Oh, you will, will you?" There was mocking menace in his voice when he rose over her, grabbing her wrists with one hand and teasing her belly with tickling fingers. Diana shrieked and squirmed, scooting backward on the bed, flipping over to protect the vulnerable target. "Who's master here?" Brock demanded.

Her shrieks subsided as Brock let her pull away from him. She peered over the side of the bed and laughed again. "Master, you left your underwear on the floor.''

Diana stretched and yawned and snuggled against the sheets in early enjoyment of the delicious morning as butterscotch sunshine spilled freely through the tall window of Brock's bedroom. Brock was not beside her now, but he'd slept next to her all night.

She turned on her side toward the place where he'd slept and inhaled the smell of him, touching the pillowcase where his head had been.

Of course he'd have gotten up early to . . . to tend the animals or prime the pump or some such morning ranch chore. She would find a robe—*his* robe—and shower, use *his* wet soap and *his* damp towel, and make breakfast for him.

The robe, the shower, the soap, and the towel were all readily available, but Diana found breakfast made. Having eaten, Brock entertained himself by watching Diana eat while he enjoyed a second cup of coffee. He liked the way she looked in his robe, so voluminous on her that she had to struggle with the sleeves to keep them out of her eggs. It may have been the shower, but he preferred to think that the love he'd made with her the night before fairly glowed in her face this morning.

"You look right pretty, ma'am," he drawled from his seat across the table. "I like your outfit."

Diana glanced down and pulled the robe together in front. "Mmm, yes, utility without style—what every practical woman is wearing this season." She flashed him a smile. "So shall we be milking the cattle this morning?"

"Not unless you wanna get kicked in your utility. Not too many range cows like to be milked. No, I thought we'd go to the fair. You interested in local color?"

"You mean old codgers, fat hogs, and prize-winning homemade jam? I imagine that kind of middle Americana can be quite therapeutic for a city girl."

"I'm more interested in the rodeo. I do a little team roping. I don't know about therapeutic, though. You feel like you're coming down with something?" He grinned at her before he took her plate. "I can take you back upstairs for some inhalation therapy. You know—heavy breathing."

Diana actually blushed.

Everything on exhibit at the fairgrounds aspired to lay claim to biggest or best. The 4-H'ers displayed projects from live animals to braided rugs that awaited the moment of beribboning. The big Quonset housing the displays was also the scene of a wild game of tag, two shrieking eight-year-olds racing around Brock and Diana as they strolled into the building. Minutes later, as they were laughing over a young boy's frantic efforts to recover his escaped pig, they heard a familiar shout.

"Daddy! Daddy!"

Turning, Brock caught Christopher in his arms midleap. "Hey, son. How was the sleepover?"

"Pretty good, Daddy. We made a racetrack for the Matchbox cars out in Jeff's sand. You gonna rope?"

"Thought I would. Diana came to see me in the rodeo. Where's Jeff?"

"Over there." Christopher pointed at the Reinharts, who stood near the open doorway. "We want caramel apples. Can you get us some?"

Brock saw to the apples while Diana saw to her second blush of the day, this time in response to Jackie's radiant grin. Jackie laughed and gave Diana a quick hug.

"Jackie . . . really!" Diana sputtered in her friend's ear, afraid for a moment that Jackie was about to congratulate her.

"I'm just glad to see you—glad you came—glad it's—"

"How 'bout an apple, Pollyanna?" Brock held the offer under Jackie's nose, and she took it with another laugh. "You guys were gone already when Diana stopped to . . . uh . . . change clothes."

"We didn't know you'd be coming to this," Jim said, nodding in the direction of the parking lot. "See you brought a horse."

"I told Wayne Dressler I'd heel for him. I haven't had much time for it yet this year. Could be a disaster."

"Somehow I doubt that." Jackie's eyes danced at Brock and then at Diana. "Brock's a terrific team roper. He won a saddle last year at the state fair."

"I had a good partner last year. Never missed a head catch. He turned pro after last season."

"Which is what you should've done," Jim said.

Brock laughed at the idea. "I don't have time for that. It's just a hobby with me. Ken was the real cowboy—just a carefree kid, nothing to do all day long but rope his dad's steers."

"Well, I think you're every bit as good as Kenny is," Jackie declared. "Heeling looks harder than heading anyway. It always surprises me that you can rope both those hind legs at once."

"There's a trick to it," Brock confessed. "And I'd better get saddled up and let my horse stretch his legs. Hey, Chris!" he called. Christopher turned at the sound of his father's voice. "C'mon, son, let's get Mr. Moon ready to chase steers."

"Can Jeff come?" Christopher asked hopefully. Brock nodded. "Can Tracy come?"

"Sure. Bring the whole neighborhood. Everybody gets a ride."

"Can I come?" Diana echoed, feeling a little foolish at the realization that she wanted to follow him back to the pickup. Brock's arm dropped over her shoulders, and she smiled.

"You can come, but you can't ride. I don't have time to fish my horse out of the drink."

The event Diana had come to see was over quickly. A long-horned steer, released from a narrow chute, made a mad dash for the opposite end of the arena, where its fellows were penned, but Brock and Wayne were hot on its heels. Wayne's loop flew from his hand first and fell squarely over the horns. The steer's own weight met the

end of the length of rope with a body-twisting bang as
Wayne's mount veered to position the catch for the heeler.
Brock's rope followed, snaking under the steer's hind legs.
When Brock pulled the slack and dallied his rope around
the saddle horn, the top line of the steer stretched between
the two ropes like a hammock, horns to hind hooves.

"Hey, that's all right!" Diana exclaimed, grinning down
at Christopher as she applauded. "Your daddy's a pretty
handy cowboy."

"I bet he won! I bet he'll let me ride Mr. Moon now."
Christopher was on his way down the bleacher incline.
"C'mon, Diana. Let's go over by the chutes. I gotta keep
an eye on you. Dad said."

"Oh, really?" Diana laughed, following the little boy.

"Yeah. You like my daddy?" The boy squinted in the
sun, expecting honesty.

"Very much."

"I like you a lot better'n Rita or Janelle. I like you a lot.
Wanna come over and see my frog? I got one in a jar."

"I used to make houses in the wet sand for my frogs
and toads. Have you ever made a frog house?" Christopher
shook his head. "We'll have to make a frog house,"
Diana concluded, and she smiled back at Brock, who was
grinning proudly in her direction as he swung down from
the saddle.

Christopher's dark-haired mopped head dropped over on
Diana's shoulder almost immediately after he was strapped
in his car seat. Making use of the shoulder strap, his seat
was by the passenger's side, leaving Diana to sit in the
middle. She balanced his head against her, stroking the
hair back from his face. Brock caught the gesture and felt
an inexplicable tightening in his chest as he watched the

delicate hand touch his son's soft, round face. Just a fleeting moment of soft on soft for his little boy.

"That's one tired kid," he remarked, bringing his eyes back to the road. "Probably didn't get much sleep last night. Still needs a nap in the afternoon most of the time. I start thinking of him as a little man sometimes, but he's still just a baby, really."

Diana looked down at the sleeping face and thought it remarkable that it took so little time to grow from that helpless state of baby, that totally dependent state. So little time; so much good fortune.

"Looks like there's a fire in the making here." Diana's head snapped in the direction Brock pointed out. It was close enough to the road that the low line of flames was visible, and the gray smoke seemed to run from the west wind's steady chase. "This wind could carry it a mile in no time. Grass is so damned dry. We have to stop, Diana." Brock turned the pickup along a gravel section-line road that brought them nearer the fire.

One other pickup had been left there, and one man could be seen beating at the flames with a blanket, while another, inside the black pickup, seemed to be using a radio. "That's Darryl Walker's pickup. He's got a two-way. Look, you stay with Chris. I've got to help out here, at least until more help comes. This is bound to spread fast."

"Of course, Brock. What can you do? Just beat the flames with a blanket? I could do that."

Brock glanced over his shoulder at the fire and then at Christopher. "If he stays asleep . . . until more people get here, maybe you could. . . ."

Diana was already releasing Christopher's seat belt and lowering him to a comfortably prone position. "Maybe we can contain it until the fire trucks get here," she said.

Brock chuckled. "This is a prairie fire, Little Rhodey. How many hydrants do you see out here? Come on, we'll go spit on it a while."

Diana glanced back through the window at Christopher before she took the saddle blanket Brock handed her and sprinted behind him toward the flames.

Chapter Six

*T*he west wind carried the flames away from the section-line road, eating up the grass steadily as it moved eastward. With only four people beating at the flames, the fire gained precious grass ground. Diana gagged at the billowing smoke when the wind gave her a mouth full of the acrid stuff. She would beat out a spot, move down the line, and watch as the last spot flared up again. Following the fire line, she drifted away from Brock, but the same aimless trail blazer brought her back within sight of him.

She couldn't see much behind the cloud of smoke. Beyond that gray curtain somewhere was the road and the charred field. She turned on her heels and looked at the field to the east. It would be destroyed. The fire crept steadily, goaded by the wind. The dry grass would knuckle under. Brock was moving closer to her, and she straightened her back, ironing out the kinks with her hand. She cast him a hopeless glance, and he strode over, pausing once to beat at a sniper of flame.

Standing close, he wiped at the soot on her cheek, but his char-dusted fingers only made the smut darker. "You okay?'' he asked. ''The smoke can really get to you.''

''My eyes are burning,'' she said.

''I know. There are a few more people on the line now. You go on back.''

''I don't see anyone.''

''They're spread out over there.'' He waved the saddle blanket toward the south. ''You go on back. Check on Christopher. Over there—see? There's a break in the fire. No grass there; it's a buffalo wallow.'' Diana looked to him again for one more statement of reassurance. ''Be careful. Watch out for . . . watch the direction of the wind. If Chris wakes up, he might get scared.''

Diana nodded and made her way toward the buffalo wallow; it looked like a huge, cracked clay dish. There was nothing in it to burn.

The smoke stung in her lungs as she trotted toward the road. Charred ruin cracked under her crepe soles. She could see several vehicles parked along the fence line, and she scanned for a blue-and-silver pickup. Her eyes were burning, tearing from the smoke.

Reaching the three-strand barbed-wire fence, Diana pushed the bottom strand down and lifted the middle one enough to slip through. As she let the bottom strand go, a barb snagged her jeans, tearing a small hole in the denim. She ran down in the ditch and up to the roadbed, then she trotted the length of the shoulder, past all the vehicles. No blue-and-silver pickup. Reversing her direction, she trotted again. Brock's pickup was not there.

Retracing her route through the field, Diana looked for Brock. Smoke attacked her eyes, retreated, swept in again, and she wasn't sure where she was until she stumbled into the buffalo wallow. She called out to him, caught a lungful of smoke, and gagged before she stumbled on.

"Diana!" Hands gripped her shoulders, and she sagged between them, coughing. "What's wrong?"

"Christopher . . . pickup's gone!" Each heave of her chest gave her a sharp stab. "I looked . . . everywhere . . . along the road."

"Somebody must've moved it. C'mon, we'll find out where."

With Diana in tow, Brock bounded down the fire line, asking each fire fighter if he'd moved the blue-and-silver pickup. Diana sighed with relief when one older fellow turned a blackened face up and nodded as he wiped his brow on his shirt-sleeve.

"Smoke was makin' your horse nervous. He was puttin' up a fuss in the trailer, so I took the whole outfit back to my place."

"What about Chris?" Brock asked.

"Who?"

"My son was sleeping in the pickup, Frank. Did you . . ." The man was shaking his head, eyes now sharing Brock's concern. "When I left . . . he was asleep on the—"

"Nobody there when I . . . But the door on the driver's side wasn't shut tight. Little fellow must've . . ."

Diana listened, watched the man's head, still shaking slowly as he pieced his supposition together, and her throat tightened.

"He must've come looking for me." Brock flicked a glance at Diana. No panic. His eyes were hard. "He's wandering around here somewhere. We've got to . . . Frank, help me spread the word!"

Those who fought to contain the fire were asked to keep an eye out for the boy. Now the fire threatened a child, and in the struggle for territory the fire was ahead of the people at this point. Brock and Diana ran calling for

Christopher, looking for spots where he might be concealed. Finally Brock pulled Diana toward the road. Breathless, they stumbled toward the black pickup that had been there when they'd stopped.

"Listen . . . Diana . . . see . . ." Brock had to catch his breath as he let himself fall against the pickup. "See if you can find a car or something with keys in it. Drive down to the highway . . . and then back north along this road. Chris may be trying to get home on foot. . . . I'm gonna try to get the police on this radio."

Diana nodded and turned her attention to the vehicles strung along the gravel shoulder. Brock reached for the door handle and jerked twice, then slammed an angry fist on the roof of the cab.

Diana gave his shoulder a reassuring squeeze. "It hasn't been that long, Brock. We haven't been here that long. He can't have—"

"Damn!" The fist came down again. "What was I thinking?" Another jerk on the door handle, and the door was torn open. "What in hell was I thinking?" he mumbled, reaching for the two-way radio.

Diana flagged a passing car and pumped control into her voice when she asked the driver whether she'd seen a little boy along the road. The woman had not, but she readily agreed to help with the search. Diana jumped onto the passenger's seat, and they rolled along the surrounding roads, keeping their eyes peeled for Christopher. They didn't see a trace of him.

Brock was no longer in the black pickup when Diana returned empty-handed from her mission. The woman in the car promised to continue the search, and Diana thanked her and headed in the direction of the fire to find Brock.

The police had come, along with two water trucks—

pickups outfitted with water tanks and hoses—and the blaze had moved farther east. As the sky darkened into evening, there was hope of containing the fire before morning. People who had been fighting the blaze had begun to help in the search for Christopher. A German shepherd was let loose on the trail, but in the smoky wake of the fire, his scenting power was ineffectual.

Still outwardly calm, Brock was methodical in his search, but Diana had begun to feel that she was searching for her own son, and she was frightened by the lengthening minutes. Standing on a knoll, charred grass under her feet, she glanced down, feeling the cold grip of doubt. The hill was bare on one side, where it looked as though it had been sliced off with a knife. There was nothing to burn there, no brush, no grass—just weathered clay, rocks . . . and one small sneaker.

"Brock! Over here! Brock!"

He made for the hill at a ground-eating trot. She watched him travel, fairly float over the black and brown. She watched him because she could not look behind her again until he came.

"There." She pointed. His eyes followed her finger, and when he saw it, he moved. Diana followed cautiously.

She slowed, stopped for a second, then felt her feet move again as she watched the big man hunker over the child, who was hidden behind a large rock. She moved toward him, stepped off the charred earth and onto the blue pile carpeting, moved nearer the crib. The back of the man's head dipped and dipped again, disappearing below his shoulders toward the little face that was . . .

Her scream stripped the skin off Brock's spine and left his nerves exposed. His head shot up as he rocked back on his heels involuntarily. Diana's hand was clamped over her mouth as if it alone had the sense to curtail her outburst. He recognized that wild-eyed look from the first time he'd seen her. It was the same stark terror.

Catching Christopher in his arms, Brock reassured his son that Daddy was there. The little boy was groggy, sooty, and he coughed once, then twice more. And then there was a stifled suffering-animal sound—but the sound wasn't Christopher's. It was Diana.

"I think . . . he doesn't seem to be hurt." Bearing his son like an infant, Brock approached her almost tentatively, the wide, wild eyes too startling, too raw, to be real. Her stance was stiff, frozen, and terrible. He spoke quietly. "I think he just . . . crawled in there and fell asleep." She managed another little anguished sound despite the hand over her mouth, four fingernails digging into her cheek.

"Diana, I said he's . . ." Brock moved carefully, keeping his voice steady. "We don't want to scare him. Come on, we'll take him into Bismarck and make sure he's okay."

"Daddy?" Diana's eyes flew to the sound of the little voice. "My throat hurts."

"I'll find some medicine for it, son."

"I didn't know where you were."

"I know you didn't. But you're okay now." The crunch of the burnt grass, punctuated by Christopher's coughing, marked cadence for the march back to the road. Dazed, Diana followed at Brock's shoulder, her face drained of all color.

"Brock!" Jackie's voice and then her body popped out of the passenger's side of their car as the soot-streaked trio reached the gravel road. Jackie hurried to meet them. "Is Christopher all right? We heard—"

"I think he's okay, but I'm taking him to the emergency room. Will you spread the word to call off the search? I want to get him over there right now."

A police car slowed to a stop beside the group. "Is he all right?" asked the driver.

"I don't know. I'm taking him . . ." Brock threw a glance over his shoulder at the parked vehicles. "I forgot . . . they moved my pickup."

"Hop in," the officer directed.

"We'll take care of the pickup, Brock," Jackie assured him.

Brock opened the police car door and then turned to Diana as though he'd just remembered. "Come with us?" She shook her head, eyes glued to the child in Brock's arms. "I could use some moral support," he added, but again she shook her head wordlessly. "You all right, Diana?" No response. He looked to Jackie for an answer.

"I think it'll be best if we take Diana home with us. You get going now." Jackie craned her neck for another look at Christopher as Brock ducked into the car. "You get to ride in a police car, Christopher! Aren't you the lucky one?" And then she whispered to Brock, "Let us know. . . ."

He nodded as he pulled the door closed.

It was late when Brock called the Reinhart house with his report on Christopher's condition. He'd been admitted to the hospital, and Brock was spending the night there with him. The boy seemed to have suffered minor effects of smoke inhalation, but the doctor wanted to watch for signs of pneumonia.

"Is Diana all right? She got pretty shook up when we first found him."

"She was exhausted. She took a hot bath and fell into bed. I couldn't get her to say much, but I could tell she was . . . Brock, did Diana tell you anything about her baby?"

"Her . . . *her* baby?"

"She didn't tell you. Maybe I shouldn't—"

"Diana has a baby?"

"No. She *had* a baby. He died very suddenly. You know . . . crib death. Happened over two years ago."

"Oh . . . geez. She never said anything."

"She hasn't really talked to me about it, either. I think she should go to the hospital tomorrow. See Christopher. She needs to."

She needed to see that Christopher was all right; Jackie was right. Her mind wouldn't function properly when she was fighting off these things. Children and death. They shouldn't even be mentioned in the same breath. There should be a law: No one dies before the age of twenty-one. No children. No babies.

Diana listened to the sound of her heels clicking against the tile floor. The rhythm of her steps was that of someone with purpose, with self-assurance, direction. Someone else was walking on her legs, she thought. Her eye sockets were an extension of the long tunnel that was the hospital corridor, and her mind retreated farther back into the dark end of the tunnel, the end that was hers, her protective corner. Someone was still walking, clicking on the tile, watching the numbers on the doors and looking for three twenty. She hadn't smelled this antiseptic cleanliness, seen this peculiarly phosphorescent whiteness, or felt this medical chill since the last day she'd been a mother.

The door was open. Brock was leaning over the sink

splashing water on his face, and a woman's voice was telling him that he needed sleep, not another shower. He rubbed a towel over his face, mumbling something into it before he looked up at the doorway. Seeing Diana, he smiled, and the warmth in his eyes drew his heart out of hiding. He came to her and folded his arms around her as though he'd been waiting for her for a long time. She hugged his waist.

"I'm glad you came."

"I'm sorry I keep flying off the handle. Just when I really need to be in control, I fall apart like an emotional fool. How's Christopher?"

"Still coughing some. His chest's been sore, but he's gonna be fine. Come on in and say hello. My mom's here," he said, pulling Diana into the room under his arm. "Mom, this is Diana Peters. Diana, this is my mother."

Brock had his mother's eyes, dark chocolate with a liquid sheen. The woman was small and attractive, dark hair heavily streaked with silver-gray. Her smile was that unspoken approval a mother offers once in a while when the woman who interests her son is obviously more than a well-proportioned bit of feminine fluff.

"I'm glad you've come, too, Diana. Maybe you can persuade my son to leave this room long enough to at least get something to eat."

"Hi, Diana."

Diana's smile for Mrs. Reed brightened at Christopher's greeting. She moved around the bed and sat beside him. "Hi, Christopher. I brought you something." A small stuffed frog emerged from her purse. "They wouldn't let me bring a real one into the hospital."

Brock touched his mother's arm. "I have a better idea,

Mom. You and I'll get some lunch while Diana visits with Chris."

"Brock," his mother admonished, "the lady didn't come to baby-sit."

"The lady came to see how Christopher is. Right, Diana?"

"I certainly did. Christopher and I have frog business to talk over. I might even know some stories."

"I might know some, too," Christopher said as his father ushered his grandmother out the door.

Diana noted the coughing. It wasn't continuous, but it came from deep in his chest. She explained to Christopher that there was probably still a little smoke in there, and his lungs were trying to push it out. "That happens to real firemen, too, you know. I heard they got the fire out completely last night, and we were practically the first ones there."

"I was bad, wasn't I?" Christopher asked, looking down at the green toy on his lap. The bed was cranked up behind him. "I should have stayed in the pickup."

"Did your daddy say you were bad?"

"No, but I heard him talking to Gramma. I made him feel bad because I got near the fire. I'm not supposed to fool around with fire."

"That's true, Christopher, but this time nobody was fooling around. Your daddy had to help stop the fire, and he thought you'd be asleep for a while. And you thought Mr. Moon was going to hurt himself, so you went to tell your dad. You just didn't know where he was. But next time you'll know that when you see smoke and fire, you must stay far away from it. And next time your dad will probably wake you up to tell you what's going on."

"I don't want Daddy to feel bad."

"Then I guess you should tell him that. Maybe your dad thinks *he's* done something bad."

Christopher shook his head over a cough.

"Does it hurt when you cough, sweetheart?"

"A little bit." Christopher mustered his most pathetic, sad-eyed look.

"Would it help if I told a story or two?" The boy nodded and settled under the crisp white sheet with a little smile.

Diana let the bed down and then launched into "The Frog Prince." Next she surprised herself by reciting some of the Robert Louis Stevenson poems she'd loved and memorized as a child. Like a lyrical lullaby, the poetry at last soothed Christopher into sleep.

Diana took her purse to the other side of the room, intent upon using the mirror.

"You have a good memory."

His voice tumbled into the quiet room and jostled her senses. He was shouldering the doorjamb, and he smiled when she looked up at him.

"How long have you been standing there?"

"Since 'The Land of Counterpane.' I loved those poems, too. And while I was sailing my mother's laundry basket on the sea of grass, I'll bet the real ocean was filling up the holes you dug in the sand."

"And we both hated to go to bed in summer when it was still light. . . . He's all right, isn't he?"

Brock pushed away from the doorjamb and closed the door behind him before taking the few steps between them. He sighed when he took her in his arms again, as though she brought him some relief after the all-night vigil. "God, I hope so. Sometimes I think I do everything wrong with him. I should have known."

"You can't anticipate every danger, Brock. It was necessary. . . ."

"When you're looking into a wall of fire, it's pretty damned stupid not to anticipate danger."

"Christopher knows you feel guilty, and that makes him feel guilty, too. There's no profit in guilt. It was a set of bad circumstances, not anyone's fault. It's over, and we have Providence to thank for . . . for the way things turned out."

Brock leaned back and looked into her face. "I've never known anyone like you, Diana. I mean that. My life's been filled with all the wrong women."

"The wrong woman gave you the right little boy." Diana was comfortable with his arms around her. "You look tired. You haven't slept at all, have you?"

He shook his head. "But my mother brought me some clothes, and I've showered and shaved, and I sure could use a kiss."

"Me, too."

His lips were soft on hers, toying with them in gentle greeting. Then he drew her firmly against him and took the kiss he needed, gave the one he needed to give, the one that told Diana how he'd felt as he stood there listening to her recite poetry for his son. And Diana returned the kiss, the essence of her heart rising to her lips to give what she needed to give. But their needs were too profound for the moment, and so, with great restraint, they kissed lightly at one another.

"Will that get you through the rest of the day?" Diana asked, curling her fingers against his back, running her fingernails up and down.

"Mmm." He smiled his satisfaction. "Not a chance.

You're addictive, sweetheart. In another hour I'll probably need a double shot.''

"And if you don't get it?"

"Withdrawal isn't a pretty sight. You wouldn't put me through that, would you?" Diana shook her head. "Good. Let's sit down and have a little talk so I can get my mind off that empty bed over there."

Diana sat on one of the two chairs in the room, while Brock pulled one over from Christopher's bedside. He obviously had something on his mind. His face was set in stone, but his eyes were soft.

"Look, Diana, if I start intruding where you don't want me, let me know, and I'll back off. I mean that—any way you want to look at it. Okay?"

"Okay." He was on the verge of something serious, something she probably didn't want to talk about.

"I don't think I've ever seen the kind of terror I saw in your eyes yesterday," Brock said quietly. "Unless it was the other time, when you . . . when Christopher ran out in front of your car."

"I know I acted like a real idiot . . . both times."

"You weren't *acting* like anything. You were terrified."

"They were terrifying moments."

"Yes, they were," he agreed. "But it was more than that, wasn't it—more than the moment?" He waited, but she said nothing. She looked down at her hands as though she'd been caught doing something wrong with them. "Tell me about your baby, Diana." Her eyes flew to his face. "Jackie told me."

She sighed and leaned back against her chair. "Then you know. Robbie died. That's really all there is to know. It's all I know. Sudden infant death syndrome. The name says it all. You have a normal, healthy baby for six

months, and then one morning you find him . . . not
breathing.'' She felt the warmth of his hand cover both of
hers, and she shot a glance in the other direction, feeling
the pinpricks of tears worrying her throat. *Not now. I don't
want this now.*

"Were you the one who found him?"

"Yes, but Doug came in behind me, and we . . . he
tried mouth-to-mouth resuscitation, and I called the ambu-
lance. Robbie breathed on his own again for a while, but
he never regained consciousness. It was in the hospital . . .
about five hours later . . .''

She looked at Brock, a hint of fear in her eyes now,
tears brimming to wash it away. "When I saw you lean
over Christopher as though you might put your mouth to
his, I thought he couldn't breathe, and then I thought . . .
I lost my sense of . . . of time and place for just a
moment. I thought I saw . . .'' She closed her eyes.

In an incomparable gesture of tenderness, Brock took
her tears, sliding his thumb over the fragile skin beneath
her eyes. And when she opened her eyes, he touched the
wet thumb to his lips. She tried to smile, but the tears only
flowed harder.

When he pulled her onto his lap and cradled her against
his chest, she knew for the first time in her life that she
needn't be afraid of her feelings. "Give them to me,
Diana. Give me all the tears. I know their value. I know
you've paid dearly for them. Give them to me, and I'll
guard them for you. No one else will see them."

She wept quietly for a time, and he held her against his
chest and absorbed the tears with his heart. When they
were spent, he tissued wet traces away from her face and
touched his lips to her hair, her eyelids, and her lips.

Finally she told him, "No one else has ever been so gentle with me."

"No one else has seen your need for gentleness. Anyone who saw it would have to respond. So much terror . . . so much pain . . . so much love . . . in one remarkably beautiful woman."

"I felt guilty for a long time. If only I'd checked on him earlier . . . maybe if I'd breast-fed him . . . I shouldn't have gone back to work part-time. Doug agreed on every point. Our marriage had been rocky anyway, and Robbie's death left us with nothing but recriminations. It took time, but I let go of the guilt. And I've let go of the crutches I used to keep up the controlled front—the tranquilizers they gave me to get through the grief, the postgrief, and the *post*-postgrief. But now, just when I think I'm all put back together again, I have another of those terrible moments. I don't know why."

"You miss your baby, Diana. That's why. He's gone, and you don't want him to be gone. You miss him. It's all right to say that."

"Yes . . . yes, I miss my baby."

There were no more words on the subject. It was enough that she'd told him, and he understood. It was enough that he held her while she allowed herself to be completely vulnerable in his presence. It was enough that she trusted him.

It took some persuading to get Brock to lie down on the empty bed for a while. He agreed to a few moments' rest, but he fell asleep quickly, leaving Diana to thumb through a magazine and watch over the two men who'd recently occupied ninety percent of her thoughts. Two weeks before, she'd not known them at all, and now she sat watching them sleep.

Such an intimate thing to do for a man. She listened to the sleep-shallow breathing in the otherwise quiet room. Christopher with his little frog, Brock with his arms folded over his chest and his booted feet clearing the foot of the bed by some inches. Both beautiful faces. Such an intimate moment to spend with a man.

"There's nothing wrong with being in love with Brock Reed, Diana. He's a fine man."

"I didn't say anything about love. Obviously I find him . . . very attractive."

"Attractive! Don't give me that worn-out adjective, Diana Peters." Jackie stopped adding to her pile of folded T-shirts to give Diana a disapproving shake of the head. "I've known you a long time, better than you realized. All the time we were in college, you never once spent the night with anybody—not even Doug. Nobody ever caught you off guard; you never lost your head even for a minute. And you never lost your heart at all."

"Not even to Doug?"

"Most certainly not to Doug. Doug was the right man on paper—had all the qualifications—but I hated to see you marry him. I expected you to say 'I do' and then shake on it. No, Diana, this is different. This . . . this is cymbals crashing and bongos beating in the jungle."

Diana giggled and gave Jackie's shoulder a squeeze. "You were always such a corny romantic. I used to chalk it up to your wholesome, midwestern upbringing, and I loved you for it. So genuine—but so naive."

Jackie clasped her hands over her heart as if wounded to the core, then laughed and gave Diana's knee a playful whack. "So what are you going to do?"

Diana took a deep breath and let it out thoughtfully.

"Well . . . I'll tell you. I thought I had happiness all figured out once. You just had to plan for it, work it into your schedule, make the most suitable arrangements, and voilà. But life hasn't gone according to plan for me. Maybe the best thing about Brock is that he wasn't anywhere on my schedule."

"I repeat: So what are you going to do?"

Diana plopped the last of the towels on the pile. "I'm going over to Brock's to see how Christopher's doing. Beyond that, I'm pleased to report that I have no plans." She gave the towels a parting pat, leaned over to offer Jackie a peck on the cheek, and headed for the door with a winsome smile.

"I thought you said Christopher was fine."

"He is! See you later." The door closed behind her.

Chapter Seven

"Hey, Diana, look! Look what I've got!"

Giving the car door a shove was an afterthought. In her sneakers and blue jeans, Diana felt like the kid who'd come to play. Returning Christopher's grin, she sat down beside him on the back step. "What have you got this time?"

"Toads!" One chubby arm thrust into a mayonnaise jar, emerging with a fist full of brown hop toad. "They're almost like frogs. Can we make a house for them?"

"Sure." Diana accommodated the toad in cupped hands, reminding herself that there'd been a time when this didn't bother her at all. "A toad house is pretty much the same as a frog house."

"I got another one." He plunged his arm in the jar, and out came a second toad. "They're brothers."

"How can you tell?"

"They look just alike, only this one's bigger, see? If I have a brother, I'll be bigger than he is, and he'll be small like this toad."

"That's true."

"I want a brother, or even a sister would be okay."

"What does your daddy say about that?"

"He says maybe someday." Christopher put his toad back in the jar, and Diana followed suit. "Someday's after Christmas, isn't it?"

"Someday is the future, and the future is like a big, shiny star. We can't touch it, but it's out there."

Christopher gave her a puzzled look and then shrugged.

"We need some sand for building houses," she added. "Is your cough all gone now?"

Christopher handed Diana his jar before scrambling down from the step. "Yeah, almost. C'mon over to the sandbox."

Diana was intent on constructing the walls of her second little sand creation, and Christopher was busy admiring the twig roof on the first miniature thatched house, when Brock caught them both by surprise. "Hello, Diana. Didn't hear you drive up."

"Diana came over to show me how to build these toad houses. Look, Daddy. See the little tiny roofs?" Christopher's delighted giggle was infectious.

Brock squatted beside the sandbox, forearms draped over his thighs, and examined Diana's work. He smiled at her bare feet and her proud grin. "She really knows how to keep her toads happy, doesn't she?"

"A toad's home is his castle," Diana quipped.

"Most women can't *bear* toads, Christopher." Brock ran a playful finger across the knuckles of five of Diana's bare toes and then threw her a wink as he added, "But Diana's a very daring lady."

"Hmm . . . Christopher, do you know what happens when you touch the soft underbelly of a toad very lightly?" Diana asked.

"What?"

Diana's lunge at Brock caught him off guard. "He croaks!" Before he could recover, Brock was pushed into the grass. "Help me, Chris!" she yelled as she planted herself across Brock's chest. "Hold his other arm!" Christopher complied, and Brock, laughing, offered only a token struggle. Diana whisked the front of his shirt from his belt and ran chilling fingernails along his hard belly.

"No!" Brock shouted, convulsing with laughter. "I can't stand that! Stop it! You'll pay . . . both of you!"

"No more awful puns. Swear!" Diana's hair hung over Brock's face as she struggled to keep him still. Christopher shrieked with glee.

"All right!" Brock laughed. "No more. . . ."

"No more double entendres. Swear!"

"I swear! I swear!"

Diana rolled off him, giggling, and Brock sat up, snatching Christopher and tousling his hair. "Turn on your old man, will you? You'll be moving your bedroll out to the barn, boy. Whew!" He cast Diana a mock-wary look. "You've discovered my Achilles' heel. I can't stand that. Turns me to jelly."

"Ah . . . well, turnabout's fair play, then."

"I'm glad you see it that way. But for the moment I propose a truce. We've got plans to make." Brock offered a handshake, and when Diana took it he drew her closer to his side on the grass.

"What sort of plans?"

"Camping plans. Chris and I want to take you out on an overnight. We've talked it over, and we think you'd make a fine camper, the way you get along with wildlife and all. Like to fish?"

"No."

"Good. We don't, either."

"Daddy, we love fishing!"

"Ever do any backpacking?" Brock continued.

"Have *you* ever done any backpacking?" she challenged.

"No. It sounds good, though. I'm trying to impress you, but I can't offer you a ride on my sailboat or a Broadway show."

"You gave me a ride on your tractor and a county fair, not to mention my very first romp in the hay. When are you planning to make this trek into the wilderness?"

"Soon as we get you to agree to go along with us."

"Is Christopher really up to this?"

"Doctor says it can't hurt him . . . unless you refuse to go and break his little heart."

Diana glanced at Christopher. "He's laying it on pretty thick, isn't he, Chris? Is this a tenting overnight?" Brock nodded. "Two tents?"

"I can arrange that."

"A lady should have her privacy."

"By all means. Is it a date?"

Diana grinned. "I do love wildlife."

Fishing wasn't as bad as Diana had thought. The Reinharts had contributed the use of their cabin tent, air mattresses, sleeping bags, and two children, and everyone but Diana was a seasoned fisherman. There was so much enthusiasm for the activity that at first Diana thought she would just play along, do the "good sport" number. The little group strung itself out along the riverbank in the low evening sunlight, and Brock, casting his own line and securing the pole on the ground, relished the role of instructor.

Standing behind her, he showed her the way to swing her pole. Then he made her cast several times before he announced that it was time to bait her hook.

"With what? Those little fish?"

"Minnows. You can't call yourself a fisherman unless you bait your own hook."

"I don't remember calling myself a fisherman, and I don't think I could shove one of those little fish onto a hook. They're alive!" Diana folded her arms over her chest and watched Brock retrieve a wiggling little creature from the cooler.

"So are the ones we're trying to entice to take the hook." Deciding not to push her, he caught her dangling hook and baited it himself.

"That's different," she protested. "If a fish takes the hook in his mouth of his own accord, that's his choice. Then he's gotten *himself* hooked."

"Sounds like female logic," he muttered. "Okay, let's see you cast it. . . . Good shot!"

"Is that far enough?"

"It is if there's a gullible fish out there."

There were three gullible walleye and a northern pike, which Diana caught and reeled in herself, squealing with delight.

Brock declared that her catch would make fine eating, better than the walleye, in his opinion. Flushed with her success, Diana even agreed to help clean the fish.

Wood smoke and fish frying in the cast-iron skillet gave the campsite an aura of authenticity—roughing it as Diana had not done before. She was drawn by the simplicity of the preparations for supper, the tantalizing odors those preparations produced, and the excitement of being self-reliant. Even coffee smelled special outdoors.

Brock sprayed mosquito repellent on the children and initiated a marshmallow roasting while Diana cleaned up what there was to be cleaned from supper. As she stood by the tailgate of the pickup scrubbing vigorously at her hands, a denim jacket fell over her shoulders, and the hands that put it there lingered. "Gets chilly when the sun goes down," he said. "You doing Lady Macbeth?"

"Just trying to get rid of that fish smell."

He sniffed at his own hands. "Yeah, I see what you mean." He reached for the soap and plunged his hands in the basin, watching her dry hers on a towel. Then she hoisted herself up on the tailgate and produced a bottle of hand lotion. "I'll have to spray you, too," he said. "The smell of that stuff'll probably draw man-eating mosquitoes."

"It doesn't have much scent. Smell." She thrust her hand beneath his nose. "Here, let me try softening yours up a little." Brandishing the towel, she took his hand and drew him in front of her. She blotted his hands dry as though they might harbor some fragility somewhere. Then she poured a dollop of cream in his palm and smoothed it over the hills and valleys of his long, beefy hand, which she cradled in both of hers, sliding her thumbs along the deep creases. Each callus received extra lotion and special circular ministrations.

No one had ever made love to his hands. He'd never thought of them as particularly sensitive in themselves, but the way she touched them, almost as though she had a special affinity just for his hands, was as exciting as any caress he'd ever experienced.

It was he who usually offered the caressing. His hands generally offered pleasure. Did she know? Did she mean to make him feel this way? He willed her to look up at him, and she responded wordlessly, her eyes liquid warmth in the cool night air. She knew.

Diana slid off the tailgate and into Brock's arms. Since he didn't step back from where he stood, she found herself wedged tightly against him. She felt the tension she'd built in his body, and she pressed herself against it as she offered her mouth up to him. The jacket dropped from her shoulders, and she heard it fall behind her on the tailgate. The little whimper that escaped her throat said welcome to his tongue.

He kissed her long and hard, delighting in the sweetness inside her mouth. He wanted to be closer to her, tightened his arms around her and couldn't get close enough. He envisioned a cocoon for two. "Could I tempt you to my fire with a few burnt marshmallows, beautiful moth?" he said, soft words against the sweep of hair on her forehead.

"Moth? Is that a . . . regional term of endearment?"

Brock chuckled. "I was thinking of cocoons for some reason. The kids'll be worn out pretty soon, and we'll get the fire all to ourselves."

"And I'll be drawn to your flame?"

"Irresistibly." He reached behind her for the jacket and put it over her shoulders again. "They'll want to bed down together and giggle for a while. We'll put them all in the big tent, and I'll . . . join them later."

"After I lose my head and dive headlong into the fire?"

"Hell of a good metaphor for seduction, isn't it?" When he draped his arm over her shoulder, she slid hers behind his waist, and they headed toward the campfire.

"Now you've given yourself away," she noted.

"I thought I did that when I kissed you."

"Daddy!" It was the voice of frustration. "Daddy, my marshmallows keep dropping off the stick."

"Mine keep turning all black," Tracy chimed in.

Brock and Diana turned their attention to the marshmallow problem. When the marshmallows were gone and the sticky hands and faces were washed, teeth brushed, and air mattresses filled, the children allowed themselves to be zipped into a double sleeping bag for the night. It was another twenty minutes before the sounds of squirming and giggling quieted within the tent.

The night air was cool and the night sky gloriously filled with a jostling crowd of stars. Rustling cottonwoods were soft background for the crackling campfire. Sitting on a blanket with Brock's head in her lap, Diana watched dream images dance in the flames.

"What would you be doing back in Rhode Island right now?"

The voice from her lap was warm and husky, and the flames were hypnotic. "I'd be reading in bed."

"Briefs and lawbooks?"

"Probably. I needed to get away from it for a while. The office was the only place I felt I had any sanity, and I'd become . . . one of the walls or something."

He pushed her back to the blanket with gentle pressure from his hand and his encroaching upper body as he shifted and followed her down. "But you'll be going back soon. Back to torts and contracts and briefs. How long can I have you, little moth? How long before you fly?"

He didn't want an answer. He wanted her mouth, and he took it, sucking sustenance from supple lips.

And suddenly Diana didn't want to think anymore—not about beginnings or endings. She kissed him, wrapping her arms around his back to hold him tight. His hand found its way under her shirt and played the slender keys of her ribs. She caught her breath when her bra slackened, and she felt his fingers cup the fullness of her breast.

She was light-headed, and it was a wonderfully free feeling, but as he moved his mouth from hers, propriety forced the words from her lips: "Somebody . . . one of the children might . . ."

"Might wake up," he finished for her, groaning as he pushed himself away. He dipped his head for one small kiss before he rolled to his feet. "And I have to douse this fire. I think there's a ban on open campfires now anyway. We're probably breaking the law here."

Diana sighed, pulling Brock's jacket around her as she sat up.

Separating the burning pieces of wood, Brock poured water over the flames in the pit he'd dug and then shoveled dirt over the hissing coals. "Now look at the sky," he said.

Diana tipped her head back. The stars loomed over her, almost close enough to touch and brighter than they'd seemed in the firelight. "Mmm, someone polished them."

"They're like this at sea," he said, offering his hand to bring her to her feet. "When I'd get homesick, I'd look to the stars and listen for the wind."

"It's pretty awesome, this prairie. Blatant natural power. At home you begin to think man has everything under control."

"Some things shouldn't be controlled." He guided her toward the smaller tent. "When you work the land, you accept that. You can't control the elements—you don't even try. You just go along with what nature gives you." He unzipped the tent flap and swept a hand in front of him, inviting her inside.

It was dark there, but her night-adjusted eyes noticed that the double-size air mattress was filled and covered with bedding. She hadn't done that. The slope of the tent forced her to duck and then sink to her knees as she heard the zipper whine around the square tent flap. She turned at the sound of another zipper and watched Brock shed his windbreaker.

Sitting at the foot of the mattress, Diana fidgeted. "Brock, we're . . . we're behaving like a couple of teenagers. There's no sense in—"

"You know what I want to do?" One of his boots was tossed aside, then the other. "I want to make a cocoon."

"A cocoon?"

On one knee in front of her, he pulled her sneakers from her feet without untying them. "Yeah. A cocoon. How sensible is that?"

Diana smiled at him and reached for the buttons on his shirt. "Not very."

"So let's forget about sense for a while and just go with what nature gives us." The buttons were undone. He shrugged out of his shirt and helped her with hers. They could see shadows, curves, outlines of one another bare to the waist. "Let's focus on what I'm going to give you . . . what you're going to give me."

Diana scooted to the middle of the bed, and Brock followed her, unfastening her jeans and uncovering the sleek, slender length of her. "I'm cold," she murmured, watching him shuck his own jeans in the shadows beyond the bed.

"Good. You'll appreciate me all the more." When he went to her she took a deep breath, and he felt her chest inflate within the circle of his arms. "Warmer?"

"You have a very warm body."

"Let me share it with you," he said. He massaged her shoulders while his mouth puffed hot breath over her breast, lips nipping softly at the curve of the underside. He teased his way to her nipple and then let his tongue and teeth create a pinnacle ripe for a grown man to suckle. She moaned, and his tongue tended to the other side, touching his first creation with gentle fingers.

Diana was lost in a maelstrom of sensation. Each kiss was a new feeling, each touch uncovered a part of her left untouched until Brock found it. His hot, wet kisses wended slowly along her breastbone. He slid strong hands along her sides to claim her hips while he nibbled at her belly. Then she tensed, realizing that this was no aimless trek, that his destination was too deeply personal to be shared that way. "Brock . . ."

He nuzzled her thigh, aware that his very breath against her tender skin made her shiver. "Shh, sweetheart. Let me give this to you." The descent of his kiss made her soar, shudder, and she bit the back of her hand lest she shout his name. Yes! her mind rejoiced. With this man, she could share. Whatever he took, he gave back tenfold.

He took her hand from her mouth. "It's all right, Diana. Talk to me. Scream at me. No one else will hear. Let me know what pleases you."

"You please me," she gasped, finding his earlobe within range of her teeth. "Everything about you is . . . I feel so inadequate now. I want . . . to be *more* for you. I want to tell you . . . show you . . ."

"Touch me, Diana. Tell me with your hands. Show my body it pleases you."

That had never been possible for her. She'd not been able to touch before. But this was Brock. This was Brock, beautiful and sensitive, and her hands loved the hard planes of his smooth chest, the long, tapering torso, the taut abdomen, and the rigidity that lay against his belly, proclaiming the need he held in check for her.

He kissed her neck and shoulders and lips, never still, breathing harder as she stroked him. It was a surprise when he rolled suddenly to his back, pulling her over him, setting her astride him and filling her with his full-blown desperation. His hands helped her find their rhythm, and then she drew him to the heights he'd pushed for. He breathed the three syllables of her name over and over in slow, adoring cadence.

Finally, in accommodation of his earlier wish, Brock zipped the two of them inside the sleeping bag and pillowed Diana's head against his chest. "I see why moths stay this way all winter," he observed, pulling her close against him so that his hand could savor all that softness.

"I don't think they ever put two into a cocoon."

"Somebody oughta tell 'em how great it could be."

"Brock, is it this great with us because . . . because you're so good at it?"

"It's great with us because we're good together." He smoothed back her hair and touched his lips to her forehead.

"I never knew . . . never imagined . . . never really . . . responded."

"I know just where to touch you, and how . . . by the way you respond. We took what nature gave us, and we made love out of it."

"The last time we were together this way, I told you I was afraid of feeling." Diana sucked in a deep breath and continued to whisper against his chin. "Now I'm afraid of what I feel. I'm afraid because 'good vibrations' doesn't begin to describe it." She waited for him to ask for an explanation, but he didn't.

"I love you," she said anyway.

Moonlight brightened the tent through its nylon screen windows. Moonlight to dress by. Brock's shirt hung open over his jeans as he pulled on the second boot. Moonlight brightened Diana's lovely sleeping face, too. Hunkering on his heels beside her, he tucked the sleeping bag around her shoulders.

Here she was. Finally the right woman had come into his life: a woman to love him, a woman who would love Christopher. This was the woman who should have been Christopher's mother. He'd known from the beginning she was a keeper—not the kind you catch for sport and then throw back in the river.

Of course they were good together; they loved each other. She was the woman he'd marry if he could. But that wasn't in the cards. And since he loved her, the last thing he wanted was to hurt her. She'd had enough of that.

He left a quiet kiss in her hair and slipped away to the children's tent.

"Listen, Diana, the man's a rancher, and he farms on top of that. This is his busiest season. When he says he can't get away, it's for good reason." Jackie turned the shopping cart around the stacks of tuna and crackers and into the canned fruits and vegetables aisle.

"I'm sure it is," Diana said. "Didn't you say you needed canned peaches for that recipe? You're walking right by them. . . . I certainly don't expect him to accept your every dinner invitation, especially when it's such an obvious ploy to throw us together."

"You're beyond the stage where anyone has to arrange to get you two together. We invite Brock for dinner quite often, and there are times when he can't make it. Simple as that."

"Yes," Diana agreed. "Simple as that."

But it wasn't that simple. Diana knew she hadn't mistaken Brock's feelings for her, but obviously she'd said the wrong words. So he'd backed off. And now, like a young girl with a crush, she had room on her mind for little else but him. This wasn't doing her any good. The time had come to head home.

Going out on the town as the third party in a group of three was not what Diana needed, either, but Jackie was adamant about entertaining her guest. So, to please her friend, Diana dressed in the flounced, country-print skirt-and-blouse outfit that Jackie'd talked her into buying that afternoon and prepared herself to be pleasant.

The parking lot was a sure indication that the Piggin String was mobbed. Jim shouldered a path for the group through the crush of cowboys grouped around the pool tables, the blackjack tables, and the bar. They were lucky to claim a table near the dance floor just as a couple was leaving it. The music was loud and swingy, and the lighting advertised every brand of beer known to man.

Jim's fingers tapped the table in time with the music as he leaned back in his chair, surveying the crowd. Then he rocked forward. "This place is pretty crowded, honey. Maybe we'd better look for someplace quieter." He glanced at Diana for agreement. "Place is short on ventilation. Too damned smoky to breathe in here."

Diana spotted the reason for Jim's sudden concern: he was sitting several tables away with a crowd of friends, leaning in the direction of the man who was talking to him and away from the woman who was apparently trying to get him to dance. "No," Diana said, "this place is fine. What I need is a good, old-fashioned eye-opener."

"Diana," Jackie objected, "those are just the guys he ropes with and their wives, girlfriends—whatever."

"I don't care who they are, Jackie, really." Diana's voice was a bit higher than normal, but that was only because the music was so loud. She opened her mouth again to tell Jackie something about Brock Reed's activities being his own business, but he walked into her field of vision, and she lost her voice. He saw her then, too, and the surprise in his face said he hadn't seen her come in.

"Diana," he said, approaching the table. "Hello. I didn't . . ."

She glanced away from him, the lump in her throat choking off any casual greeting. Her face felt hot, no doubt embarrassingly red. How ridiculous! She heard him greet Jim and Jackie, and then he passed by the table. She waited a minute before casting a furtive peek at the dance floor. He was dancing with Rita, the woman who'd intruded on their first date.

Diana found her voice. "I guess you're right, Jim. It is pretty crowded here. I think I'd like to find a quieter place."

Jim and Jackie nearly tripped over each other as they hastened to whisk her out the door. They did find a quieter place, where they had drinks and listened to soft guitar music. Diana told herself not to brood in front of these two good friends who were trying so hard to please her.

In the privacy of her room, though, she allowed time for brooding. So he'd had good reason to decline Jackie's dinner invitation. Well, maybe. He had other friends, other interests. The fact that she wouldn't be there much longer was no reason for him to suspend his usual activities "for the duration." And she wouldn't be there much longer. She had a job to get back to. She had no business falling in love with some . . . North Dakota cowboy, for heaven's sake.

"Diana . . ." Jackie tapped at the door, then swung it open. "Still awake?"

Jackie wore her robe and slippers, but Diana had only kicked off her shoes. She was sitting on the floor, her back against the bed, and her mood was clearly as blue as the bedspread behind her. Jackie set a tray on the floor beside her and settled herself on the rug.

"Hot chocolate and Oreos," she announced. "Interested?"

"No." Diana sighed and reached for a cup and a cookie. "I'm not interested in anything. I'm regressing, Jackie. I'm a sixteen-year-old who just saw her boyfriend at the dance with another girl."

"Diana, he wasn't with another girl." Jackie emphasized every other syllable as though she were scanning a line of poetry. "I keep telling you, he was obviously just out with a group of his friends—his roping buddies."

"And the local version of the Dallas Cowboys cheerleaders." Diana sipped her hot chocolate. "Oh, I'm just being ridiculous. I let myself forget several of my most sacred maxims. To wit: Never lose control of any situation. Never tell a man you love him, and *never* fall for anybody who lives in the exact middle of the continent."

"Did you really tell him you loved him?"

"I did. I do, and I did. It seemed the thing to do at the time. It wasn't, as you see."

"He cares for you, Diana. I know he does. Brock's pretty cautious, too. If you'd known his wife, you'd know why."

"Jackie, I'd have to be out of my mind to allow myself to fall in love with anyone who lives out here. It's too wide open, too wild—"

"It's not *wild*. Be fair, now . . . except maybe in the winter. Wait'll you get a taste of the winters."

"I have no intention of tasting your winters." Diana sipped again. "Your hot chocolate is pretty good, though."

Her sigh introduced several moments of thoughtful silence between the two.

The scratching on the window screen behind them gave them a start. They looked at one another, alarmed. "Diana," a voice said quietly. "Diana, I know this is your room, and I know you're in there, 'cause this is the only light on in the house."

Jackie covered her mouth to stifle a giggle. Diana rolled her eyes, silently scolding her heart for leaping imprudently. "He must be out of his mind," she said quietly, then frowned at another thought. "Out of his mind or drunk."

A forefinger flew to Jackie's lips. "Shh," she mouthed. "I'm not here." She scootched down beside the bed.

"Can he see in the window?" Diana whispered.

Jackie shook her head. "Ground slopes out there."

"Well, I'm not about to hold a conversation at the bedroom window."

"Diana! I wanna talk to you." His whisper was absurdly exaggerated.

"Call me tomorrow, then," Diana answered, injecting a note of boredom into her voice.

"This won't keep. C'mon over to the window."

"This is no way to pay a social call, Mr. Reed."

"You want me to wake up everybody in the house? I will if you don't come over here and talk to me."

Wide-eyed, the two women were quiet, trying to determine the meaning of the rustling sounds outside. There followed a thud and a grunt and a couple of choice words.

"Brock, what are you *doing* out there?"

"I was trying to reach the window—fell off the damned tricycle." Both women shook with silent hysteria. "Get over here, Diana, before I beat the door down."

"Try huffing and puffing." Diana flicked off the night-stand lamp, plunging the room into darkness.

"That's for wolves, princess. I'm just a toad, remember? What're you doing?"

"Turning the light out so I can see what's below my window in sheep's clothing." Diana scooted across the bed while Jackie slipped out of the room with a whispered "Good night, all."

Sure enough, there was a tricycle out there, along with a long-legged character sitting on the ground, arms draped over his knees, cowboy hat cocked back on his head, just basking in the moonlight.

Diana couldn't help giggling. "Did you have a good time tonight, cowboy?"

"Hell of a good time, princess. But I wanna explain something to you, so c'mon out here."

"I suppose I could let you in."

"I don't wanna come in. It's nice out, and I want you to come out."

"Don't be silly. Go on home and sleep it off."

"I've got something to say to you, and I'm not leaving 'til it's said. You want me to make a scene out here?"

"I'd rather you wouldn't."

"Besides, I can't go home. Wayne was driving tonight. I told him to let me off here."

"Where's Christopher?"

"At my mother's. Think I'd leave him—"

"No, I didn't. I'll be out in a minute."

"Bring a sleeping bag. It's kinda chilly."

"I will not bring a sleeping bag!" she hissed, throwing a sweater over her shoulders and slipping her shoes on. She grabbed her purse on her way out.

·

Brock waited on the deck, leaning against the railing. "Goin' out again?"

"I suppose I'll have to take you home. It would've been so much simpler if you'd let Wayne take you all the way to your door."

"It's been botherin' me—and Wayne agreed—best thing is to get it settled and go to bed with a clear conscience—especially after you left the Piggin String in such a huff."

"I did not leave in a huff. The crowd was just too . . . too pressing. Jim suggested a quieter spot."

"*Too, too pressing*. That's good, Diana. Bette Davis couldn't have said it better. Sure you weren't mad?"

"Why should I have been mad?" she asked in a clipped voice.

"Because I was with Rita."

"I have no—"

"Only I wasn't with Rita, and that's what I came to tell you." He stood away from the railing and took two steps, his boots clomping on the hardwood deck, and then he was right there, hands heavy on her shoulders. Her drumbeat picked up its tempo. "I wasn't with Rita. I didn't ask her out. I was with a bunch of people, a bunch of guys I rope with. She was there watching us rope, and she came along afterward."

"You don't have to explain any of this to me," she offered quietly.

"I know I don't." He lowered his head toward her.

She turned her face away. "Are you drunk, Brock? You must be to come over here like this."

"I must be." He caught her chin in one hand and closed his mouth over hers, sharing his intoxication. And Diana, drinking deeply, slid her arms around his waist and stepped in close to him. "Drunk or crazy," he muttered against her lips.

"The former for you, the latter for me," Diana acknowledged before she opened her eyes, thinking, *Crazy, crazy, crazy.*

"Why don't you take me home, then? You can make me some coffee, and I'll . . . roll out the couch for you." He gave her lower lip a quick kiss and gave her a quirky grin.

"I'll take you home since I can't get rid of you any other way. You'll have to make your own coffee, though. I don't trust drunken cowboys."

He opened her car door for her, making a point of the fact that he was still "a perfect gentleman." Then he blew it when he tried to fold his legs under the little dash in the passenger's seat. "Where the hell are you s'posed to put your legs in this thing?"

"You're supposed to be . . . shorter," she said dryly.

For five miles he worked hard at not riling her, and when she pulled up in front of his house, he sat quietly for several moments. "I've got more talking to do, Diana. I'm pretty glib after a few drinks. Why don't you just shut the engine off and come on inside?"

"It's late," she informed him, knowing that wouldn't settle it.

"Yeah, I know. Look," he began, turning toward her as far as he could in the little space that was afforded him. "I've got this problem of logistics."

"Again?"

"Right. First of all, now that I've got myself wedged into this dune buggy, I don't know if I can get out. Second, I can't decide whether to continue to sweet-talk you or to move on to manhandling you at this point."

"I must've missed the sweet talk. When was that?"

"I thought groveling at your bedroom window was pretty sweet."

"That was sweet?"

"Damn sweet."

"So what's third? There's always a third."

"Third," he continued, snapping off the ignition and taking out the keys. Then, in a quieter voice, "Third, we're wasting gas here. And I don't know what you're so mad about."

"We can talk about it tomorrow, Brock, when you're sober and I'm sensible."

He pocketed the keys. "If I tell you where I keep the crowbar, you think you can pry me outta this thing? It's a little tight . . . and that's all I am, too—a little tight."

She sighed. "And all you want is coffee?"

"Coffee and talk."

"Sweet talk?"

He gave her a tentative smile. "Coffee with sugar."

Chapter Eight

"Coffee," Diana announced, handing Brock a steaming mug. "Now talk so I can have my keys back."

"Aren't you having any? You made enough for six people."

"You wanted coffee. What are you doing?"

He was taking another mug from the cupboard. "In case you change your mind. We'll go in the family room where it's more comfortable."

"Why do I have the feeling I don't want to get any more comfortable with you? I have to have cream and sugar in that." She accepted the mug but held it away from her as though there were something distasteful about the coffee in its present state.

"No problem," he said, taking down a sugar bowl and a jar of creamer from the cupboard.

She followed him into the family room and left space between them when she sat on the couch. "So . . . you said you had a good time tonight." Why not? Might as well get down to cases.

He nodded, slurping a little as he drank from his mug.

"Mmm . . . hot. Roped some steers over at Wayne Dressler's. Bunch of us decided to head over to the Piggin String afterward. You should've stayed. We could've . . . danced."

"You *were* dancing. You were surprised to see me, weren't you, Brock?"

"I didn't expect you'd be at the Piggin String tonight. Yeah, I was surprised." He leaned back, hooking an elbow over the back of the couch.

"And not particularly pleased. A little embarrassed, in fact."

"Diana, I told you I wasn't out with Rita."

"Then why did you give me that guilty look?"

He looked her straight in the eye. "It wasn't because of anything I was doing with Rita."

"You'd decided to stop seeing me, hadn't you?" she challenged in her quiet, sensible, conversational tone.

"No . . . not completely."

"I told you how I felt the other night, but it wasn't what you wanted to hear, was it? All you really want is one night at a time." Her conversational tone had evaporated, but she was hanging on to quiet and sensible.

Brock laughed. "Honey, you must be blind."

That took care of quiet, and probably sensible. "Until recently, I saw clearly. I thought clearly, and I acted only with absolute prudence."

"Jurisprudence?" He couldn't resist.

"*Prudence* prudence. Discretion. I used to know what that meant, and, believe me, I will again."

"Okay, Diana," he began, holding up one hand in a bid for a truce. "You're getting a little angry here, and I don't want you to be angry, so I'm gonna do something really stupid. I'm gonna tell you the truth and nothing but, so

help me. Not that I've been lying, but there's more to it."
He took a deep breath, as though he were about to sub-
merge himself in something. "I knew what you thought
when you saw Rita and me together, and I was gonna let
you go right on thinkin' it. But when we got to the
Reinharts', I told Wayne to let me out. He got a real kick
out of that one."

"Am I supposed to derive something from that gesture,
or should I get a real kick out of it, too?"

He'd had enough. The mug clicked against the coffee
table glass, and he leaned in her direction, his jaw set.
"You were right, Diana: I intended to back off. I have a
five-year-old son who's as crazy about you as I am. I'd
have to be the worst kind of fool to be in love with a lady
lawyer from Rhode Island." With firm hands he turned
her by her shoulders to face him, eyes boring into hers.
"But here's a kick for you, Counselor. I'm in love with
you, sure as hell. Let's see what you derive from *this*
gesture."

With the pressure from his kiss, her head dropped back
like an oven door, and the fire that broke from his mouth
to hers was a combustion of impatience and alcohol and
the need to make her believe him. There was a moment
when she couldn't move, wedged as she was under his
mouth and between his powerful hands, but then he wrapped
his arms around her shoulders, and his mouth softened.
His lips moved over her mouth, wordlessly phrasing and
rephrasing the claim he'd just made.

Diana's consciousness was bombarded with reverbera-
tions of "I'm in love with you." She curled her arms
around his back and her tongue against his for every bit of
contact she could have with him in that moment. He
lowered her head to the pillow that was propped against

the arm of the couch, and he assaulted her face with kisses. She was drowning, gasping for breath, and he stopped to look at each part of her face, touching with his fingertips.

"Brock . . . Brock Reed," she marveled, smoothing the black hair spilling over his forehead. "Such a strong name. Two hard, solid syllables. A no-nonsense name. Where's *your* prudence, Brock Reed?"

"I'm holding her in my arms," he said, tossing the loose back cushions on the floor behind the couch to give himself a wider berth. "Prudence Peters. Very sensible girl. Doesn't trust drunken cowboys. Can't figure how she came to love one."

"I shouldn't have told you," she said, catching her lower lip between her teeth.

"Here, let me do that for you." His head dipped in for a taste of lower lip, which he eased from her teeth with his own. "Mmm . . . tender. I shouldn't have told you, either. Wasn't going to, but you made me mad with all that lip you were giving me. Thought you had it all figured, didn't you?"

Diana's eyes sparkled like green river water. "If I didn't give you any lip, you'd just take it, anyway. Want some more?"

"Just this kind," he murmured, nipping at her lips with his before descending on her with the full impact of a demanding mouth. Suddenly breaking off the kiss with a groan, he rolled to his back, reversing her to the upper position. Her hair was tossed over her face in the process, and he laughed as he whisked it back with his hand. "Don't hide from me, Prudence. Let me look at that classy face. And don't give me that smug look, either. I

liked the way those green eyes danced for me just then—
the way they do whenever you tease me.''

She giggled at him, a sound that reminded him of a little
girl. The beautiful lady lawyer had a little girl inside her.
''Truth is,'' he went on, ''I felt like a *real* toad when I
watched you walk out of the Piggin String with the
Reinharts.''

''And when I saw you with that woman, I thought for
sure I'd made a real fool of myself when I told you I loved
you.''

''Guess I sort of evened things up for you, acting like a
jackass over here tonight.''

''You didn't act like a jackass! That was a very sweet
thing you did. Nobody's ever done a balcony scene for me
before. The tricycle was a nice touch.''

''Yeah . . . well, just don't ever tell anybody about
that.''

''Not even Jake?''

''Especially not Jake.''

She smiled mischievously, enjoying the knowledge that
there had been one other witness, and someday when they
were all old and gray, they'd take out this memory and . . .
On what occasion? That of her next thirty-year visit?
''Well, I've done your bidding, Mr. Reed. It's time you
turned over the keys to my dune buggy.''

''Can't do that. You might take off in it.''

''You've had your coffee and your talk. You said—''

''I said coffee with sugar. But I don't like sugar in my
coffee. I like it on the side.'' Hands cupping her jaw, he
guided her mouth back to his.

Brock rolled in his sleep, uncomfortable on his side,
uncomfortable on his back, and not much better on the

other side. And on the other side . . . his bed was empty. Hadn't they just been together . . . or was that . . . ? His ears came to life when a distant rumble nudged at them, and then he knew the cause of his discomfort—a dull ache in his head. Hooking an arm under his pillow, he let one eye pop open at a time. A soft white figure stood in front of the window.

It was still dark outside. Brock glanced at the clock: four-thirty. Another rumble, this time a little closer. The lady who should have been warm against him in his bed was standing at the window, her back to him. Her full, white satin slip fairly glowed in the dark like some luminous figurine. He watched her shift her weight from one foot to the other, her hip now favoring the right side, the roundness of her bottom more pronounced by the sheen of the fabric that curved over it. She crossed her arms in front of her and ran her hands up and down them.

"Cold?"

She bolted, sucking a surprised little gasp.

"Sorry. Didn't mean to scare you, honey. Anything wrong?"

"It's going to rain," she said without turning.

"Good. That's exactly what we need—a two-day soaker."

"I heard the thunder."

"Scare you?"

She shook her head. "I got up to check the windows. This isn't my house. I don't know what I'm doing checking windows."

She was crying.

He threw back the covers and let his feet find the floor for him, his eyes glued to her back. "What is it, Diana?"

The instant he had her in his arms, the thunder cracked close by, and she shivered against him. He held her there and waited, his cheek resting against her hair as he turned his face toward the window. The wind was picking up. Chris would be running in here, crawling into his bed. Good thing Chris was at his grandma's. "Why are you crying?"

"The thunder woke me," she said, swallowing to soothe the foolish burning in her throat. "I didn't know where I was at first . . . and I was naked . . ."

"So am I. We made kind of a nice pair." He stroked her back, wondering if she'd had a dream. " 'Til you put this on."

"It's all I . . . I don't usually . . ."

"We slept together before like this. What happened, Diana? Were you dreaming?"

"I don't know. I'm all disjointed . . . pieces of me here, pieces there. I'm sleeping in your house like . . . like some woman who just . . . comes to your bed for the night. I didn't know where I was at first." The last of her words dissolved in her tears.

He waited the moment it took for her to grow quiet. "I don't have women coming to my bed for the night, Diana. I haven't brought anyone here since . . . since my wife. You're not here on a whim; you're here so we can be together. We both need that."

"Yes," she whispered, "we do."

The sound of wind *whoosh*ing through the trees and the *plunk—plunk—tat-tat-tat* of the first drops of rain filled in for their silence. Quick brightness followed by thunder's clatter left Diana shivering again.

"Come back to bed. Let me make love to you in the early-morning rain."

She closed her eyes and brushed her lips over his chest. "Yes, Brock. Love me through the rain."

The room was softly graylit, the sky spilling sheets of water against the windows as the two who truly were lovers explored one another in the pristine white expanse of the big bed. Brock resisted the urge to trespass against the satin slip, for she was naked beneath it, and he loved the way she felt, the way the bit of satin slipped over her skin under his hands.

She loved it, too, but when her skin tingled too much to allow the barrier any longer, she squirmed to be free of it, and his hands freed her. His tongue cleansed her, and his perfect body rinsed the world away.

"You'll sleep a little while now?" he asked later.

She surfaced, buoyed by wonder. "Maybe . . . or maybe I'll hold you while you sleep." There was a rumbling in the distance again, and Diana snuggled closer in the pocket Brock made for her with his arms. White sheets, white blanket—it was like cuddling with him inside an eggshell with the rain or some hen's beak tapping on the outside.

"Thunder bothers you, doesn't it?"

"Not exactly. Rain does sometimes. It makes me feel lonely—sort of cold and isolated, a bedraggled little animal. But this morning it's different. I could lie here all day and just wallow in this feeling. What's the opposite of lonely?"

"Love."

"Rain sounds good when you're comfortable and cozy and wallowing in love."

Brock wondered what had happened to his headache. "Wallowing in love?" He chuckled. "Pretty strange picture just popped into my head. If it means lying here with you all day long, I'm all for wallowing."

"You get to play when it rains."

"Yeah," he said, sliding around so he could prop himself on his elbow and look at her. "I get to play. Baby, you are one sweet playmate. Are you feeling better now?"

Diana nodded, lifting a forefinger to trace the line of his jaw. "Now I see what all the fuss over sex is about. Whatever was bothering me before doesn't hold a candle to what I feel right now." She remembered how sex with Doug had changed nothing inside her. Doug's kisses had left her feeling as empty as she'd been before. He had never really touched her.

"The prospect of your leaving hangs over us like the blade of a guillotine, and the tension builds until we make love. That seems to loosen things up between us," Brock said.

"But nothing's changed. The prospect still hangs there."

"When we make love, nothing matters but two people in the present. It's too intense a moment to let anything interfere." He smoothed her hair against his pillow, loving the fine-spun feel of it. "I guess that's the difference between making love and just having sex," he considered. "When you make love, you make a bond. We're changed by it, Diana. We're part of each other. You won't go without taking me with you and leaving part of yourself behind."

"It's so much more than I came with," she said, and he gathered her close again.

Chapter Nine

*H*eat and light penetrated every cell in Diana's body. The red glow beneath her eyelids precluded any real thought, certainly not while her brain simmered in its own juices. She was about done on this side; time to turn over on her back.

"Hey, Diana, it's Brock on the phone. He wants to know if he can pick you up at seven."

Diana rolled her head and squinted up at the kitchen window. She couldn't see Jackie, but the voice was there. "What for?"

"Your date."

"What date? He hasn't asked me for a date." Her eyes protested, rolling shut.

Pause. "Diana, Brock wants to know if you'll go out with him tonight." Pause. "The Piggin String. He thought you might want to try it again."

"What time?"

Pause. "He wonders if seven would be appropriate?"

"Tell him I'd be delighted, and seven would be grand."

Pause. "He says come as you are."

Her hand slid over her hip. She only wore this skimpy outfit for backyard sunbathing. On the beach she was one-piece conservatism. "Tell him—"

"I told him you'd look great in whatever, and he agreed. Sit up and have some tea with me."

Diana shaded her eyes and sat up, clicking the arms of the webbed lounge chair as the backrest followed her to an upright angle. She reached for the proffered glass. "What do you know about Brock's ex—Lori?" she asked idly.

"She was a mistake. I'm sure they'd have gone their separate ways sooner if it hadn't been for Christopher. For his sake, I guess, Brock thought he had to . . . try harder. That last summer—they were living here with his folks then. Brock was planning to go to law school that fall." Jackie pursed her lips and shook her head.

"Lori wasn't your kind of people?"

"Lori wasn't *anybody's* kind of people. She didn't like anything about her life here—wanted no part of motherhood—ran away twice that summer. The first time, Brock brought her back. The next time . . ." Jackie shrugged. "Frankly, I think she was a little crazy. Had the temper of a banshee."

"That man's had his share of off-balance people in his life." Diana gestured with a tilted hand. "Why didn't he see me coming and take cover?"

"He probably couldn't resist your bongos," Jackie teased, slanting a squinty grin, "or your bosoms, one of the two."

"Two of the four?" They giggled. "Can't boast much in the bosom department. It has to be the bongos. I've had many compliments. 'Nice set of bongos on Peters,' they say."

"Well, whatever those are bulging over that little top, they're getting mighty pink, girl. Playing any music on them tonight could be downright painful."

Diana snatched up the blouse she'd dropped beside her on the grass. "You worry about keeping your piano in tune, dear. The percussion section is always a bit hotter than the rest."

The Piggin String throbbed with the beat of the bass guitar and the heartfelt wail of the lead singer's lyrics. Their little out-of-the-way table sported a small kerosene-style lamp with a candle burning in it. Brock and Diana were sitting on a bench styled like a buckboard seat. The crowd looked remarkably the same as it had nights past—the cowboys and cowgirls, both dressed in jeans and boots, along with the sportcoat-and-summer-dresses clientele, who came for a little taste of spirit with their spirits. Brock and Diana were a mixed couple.

The dance floor was crowded, but Diana enjoyed watching the jostling dancers, colored balls popping inside the dome of a child's push toy as the band leaned on the tempo. She nursed the sweet-tart daiquiri and smiled as she studied Brock.

He looked like sweet love, his eyes warm liquid, his mouth moist, having just sipped at his beer. Diana's stomach tumbled.

Brock pursed his lips for a moment, then smiled. "Why are we sitting here when we could be alone together at home?" His fingers found her neck underneath the fall of wheat-colored hair. "Come home with me."

"I don't know, Brock," she said quietly as she watched her own hand fold the corners of her cocktail napkin. "It's becoming so complicated between us."

"So good between us."

"Too good. We're setting ourselves up for some sadness when I leave."

"Would you rather it hadn't happened?"

"No."

"When I knew for sure how I really felt, I thought . . . 'Well, hell, you'll make some memories together, and after she goes' . . . after you go, I'll still love you. But I can live with that. It's a lot more than I had before."

His other hand lay on the table beside the bottle of beer, and she reached for the long fingers, touched his knuckles, then turned his hand over in her own like a turtle to its back. Her fingers sought his palm.

"You want to make love to my hand again? Be my guest," he offered.

"Shall I read your palm?" Her fingertips smoothed the creases with care, as though preparing the surface of a medium about to receive an artist's attention.

"You can do anything you want to my palm."

"This is your life line," she began. "It's long."

He leaned close to her and lowered his voice. "In fact, what you're doing right now is one hell of a turn-on, lady."

"This is your marriage line. It's multiple."

"If I lose control, my lawyer will certainly call this an act of seduction," he growled as she ran the edge of her pink nail through the middle of his palm, sending shivers up his arm.

"Your love line is very . . . complex and irregular."

"So's my pulse rate."

"The indications of intelligence are rather . . . sparse. You are a powerful swimmer with good spring in the legs."

"It's not easy being a toad all the time."

"You'll travel in the near future."

His hand closed around hers. "And I'm taking you with

me. I've got to get you out of here—take you somewhere
for a kiss." He leaned close again. "I need a kiss, Diana."

"Tired of hopping from pad to pad?"

"Yeah, I guess I am." It was only a joke, but she could
tell immediately that she'd struck a serious chord with
him. He straightened and stared at their clasped hands.
"I'm tired of hopping in circles like somebody pulled off
one of my legs."

"I'm ready to go," she said quietly.

"Do you mind if we stop at my house for a few
minutes?"

"No, that's fine." He'd been quiet, lost in thought
since they'd left the bar, and Diana wondered whether he
was going to tell her what was bothering him.

Brock parked the pickup behind the house and handed
Diana down from the cab. He tipped the bench seat forward and reached behind it, where a storage pocket held a
denim jacket, which he pulled out and draped over her
shoulders. She flinched a bit. "What's wrong?" he asked.

"Sunburn."

He smiled, and she felt a quick sense of relief. "I
noticed you were blushing a lot tonight. It's pretty. Your
pink nose is pretty."

"Pretty tender. What's this for?" She shrugged under
the jacket.

"We're going for a walk down by the creek. Got something to show you."

Beyond the yard was a shelterbelt of cottonwood trees,
which sloped to a creek bank. The sky was an inky canopy
bright with stars, which would fade soon as morning approached. Diana followed Brock as he searched through
the tall grass. She felt something snag her panty hose at

the ankle, and when she pulled, the run scurried up her leg like a little bug. She wasn't dressed for midnight brush popping.

"Here it is," he announced.

It was a crumbling cement foundation that stood on a rise above the creek bed. *He wanted her to see this in the middle of the night?*

"My grandparents lived here. They built this little house themselves. It burned down, and they built the big house. See that hill, that place where it's dug out?" Diana peered past his pointing finger and nodded. "My great-grandparents lived in a soddy that stood there. It was sod on three sides and hill in the back. My grandfather brought me down here when I was about eight years old, and he talked about how this little frame house seemed like a palace after that soddy. Can you imagine what that was like when it rained? God—a mud hut.

"Anyway, my grandfather said it was all worth it. The house doesn't matter. Your roots are in the ground, he said. I guess he was pretty young when they came over from Germany and homesteaded. Their name wasn't Reed, but my grandfather said the guy at Ellis Island couldn't spell worth a damn, so he shortened it up for them. I don't even know what it was—started with an R and had a couple of umlauts. I asked him to write it down for me, but he wouldn't. 'Reed is a good American name,' he said. 'Your father fought for this land—American land— and we are Americans. We don't look back.' He died when I was twelve." Brock sat down on the foundation of his grandfather's house. "I hope he knows I'm still here."

Diana pulled the big jacket around her shoulders and eyed the cement ledge where Brock sat. Her soft apricot sheath would suffer, she knew, but she joined him when he gestured for her to have a seat next to him.

"There are a lot of things I'd like to do in my life, but leaving this land is not one of them. I wanted to see the world, so I joined the navy. But I came back here and brought a new wife with me. As soon as she hit North Dakota, the honeymoon was over, but I kept telling myself she'd adjust. She'd take to it like my mom did. But she didn't, and finally one day she just took off with some trucker.

"But I had Christopher. I look at my son now, and I understand what my grandfather meant about roots. Do you understand, Diana? I'm giving you this big history because I want you to understand how it is with me."

"I'm not sure . . . what it is I'm supposed to understand."

"That I'm planted here. You're supposed to understand that a North Dakota rancher is *planted* a long way from a Rhode Island lawyer. You're a cosmopolitan girl, and I'm a country boy. Have you thought much about what that means?"

"Yes," she answered, glancing at the pink hints in the sky before facing the worry in his eyes. "It would be simple if we were kids, just out of school. Neither of us would have any real time invested in anything, and we could invest it all in each other. But I've got a career, and you've got a home and a business here, and a son. We knew it wouldn't be simple if we let ourselves get . . . involved."

Brock's sigh was heavy. He let his hand drop to his thigh with an audible slap. "Simple is when a woman says 'Come on over to my place,' and I go over there, have a couple of drinks, jump in the sack with her, say 'Thanks a hell of a lot,' and go home. No big deal. That's how I spell relief.'' He gave her a long look. ''But not with you. I want to hold you against me all night long, and I don't want to let you go in the morning. In the morning, I want us to putter around the kitchen together and tease and talk, and I don't want to let you go . . . ever!''

It suddenly occurred to Diana that that was all right, and her eyes asked him what was wrong with that. Why did he have to let her go?

''I have no right, Diana. I have no damned right!''

''Loving me gives you the right.''

He stood abruptly and took three steps from her, thrusting his hands in his front pockets. Without turning around, he said quietly, ''It should have been a safe bet. A satisfying two-week relationship. Let myself really feel something for two weeks. Then when the time was up . . .'' He turned to face her. ''When the time was up, you wouldn't want to go, and I wouldn't want you to go, but we'd both know how it had to be.''

''And I'd write, and you'd call—less frequently as time went by—and after a while we'd . . .''

The word *forget* was never spoken.

''It's not gonna work that way, Diana. I didn't plan to love you this much, and I didn't plan on you loving me. I tried to stop seeing you, but I couldn't do that, either. I don't want to lose you.''

''Then why haven't you asked me to stay?''

He stood there quietly, studying her face. He hadn't expected her to say that. The sky was brightening quickly, and he could see the trust, misplaced in himself. She'd put her heart on the line, and God! how he wanted to be worthy.

''Because I can't offer you what I know it would take to

make you stay. You're the woman I want to be married to, the woman I should be married to. But I'm not. I'm . . . I'm still married to Lori.''

The sun hit the horizon like a cannonball.

Chapter Ten

"*I*'m sorry, Diana."

In the gray light he could see that her body had become as rigid as the cement she was sitting on, and the look in her eyes made him feel sick. "People assume I'm divorced. I knew that was what you'd been told, and I let you go right on thinking it."

"That's a practiced ploy, I believe." Her voice sounded hollow in her own ears. "It sounds like you've used it before. It's called deliberately misleading the—"

"At the time I guess I called it leaving well enough alone. But no matter how I stretched it around in my mind, I couldn't call it honest. Jake gave me hell for it, too."

"So you've been properly chastised, then," she said with careful steadiness. "You've been told it's a lie to omit the truth. You'll probably never commit that little sin again."

"I know this sounds crazy, but I haven't seen her for nearly four years, and I feel divorced."

"Divorced is not a feeling, Brock. It's a legal status."

"So is the custody of a child."

She looked at him, incredulous. "Then you've never gone to court over . . . any of this?"

He shook his head. "In the beginning Lori called me a couple of times, wanting money, which I sent to Denver and points west. When I mentioned divorce, she mentioned custody, so I backed off. I haven't heard from her in at least three years. I don't even know where she is."

"Brock, that's desertion. If you can't find her, you're due for divorce by decree."

"I know all that. I've talked to my lawyer about it." He cocked a wry smile. "My *other* lawyer. My wife is a bitch, but right now she's a sleeping one. And the old adage says to let sleeping dogs lie. That's what I'm doing."

"What you're doing is—" She stopped short of an accusation. Diana's anger receded for the moment, overshadowed by her indignation with a situation that was the reverse of most cases she had come across. Brock's life was being kept on hold by a woman who had left him with an infant son. "After all this time you can't think she'd want Christopher. No court in the country— "

"Don't give me 'no court in the country,' Counselor. Every time I hear about a custody case, the judgment scares me. In this part of the country, women get the kids—that's the unwritten rule. That's why men are kidnapping their children all the time. I don't know where Lori is or what she's doing, but I wouldn't put it past her to come up with some psychiatrist who's been treating her or sleeping with her or some damn thing, and who'll swear she's ready to be a model mama."

"You've seen too many movies."

"Maybe. But this is my son we're talking about here. *My son.* Up until now, my freedom didn't matter much. I just wanted her to leave us alone. I prayed she'd never try to take him back just to punish me."

"Punish you . . . for what?"

"For bringing a cosmopolitan girl into the country and making her barefoot and pregnant." The tilted mouth, arched brows, and vacant eyes resigned Brock's memory to a debit column in some tally of mistakes he was keeping for himself.

"I'm not like Lori."

"I know you're not."

"Anyway, she's not in the country anymore—we can probably assume that much—and she doesn't have any kids to worry about. Why would she—"

"Good question. Why *would* she?" He slammed a fist on his knee, then jumped to his feet and whirled to face Diana. "Why would she do anything she's done? Why did she marry me? God, I was a jackass! She was beautiful and sweet, and I was . . . stupid. Lonely, I guess. She hated me from the minute she found out she was pregnant. To this day I don't know how it happened. She must've forgotten to take a pill or something. You should have heard her cuss me out in the delivery room. Called me every damned filthy name in the book."

"She was in pain," Diana reminded him.

"Yeah, well, the pain went away, thank God, and left me a son."

"A good attorney should be able to get you full custody of Christopher," she said evenly.

He sat beside her and touched her cheek with hesitant fingers. When she didn't respond in kind, his hand dropped away. "You're the one who should cuss me out, Diana. Damn me for the coward I am. Christopher's so young. I'm the only parent he knows. I'm afraid to take any chances right now."

"I think you'd better take me back to Jackie's."

*   *   *

Diana spent two days trying to recover the old mind-over-matter outlook she'd once perfected. Perfected, nothing. Whenever she *thought* she had it down pat, she got overconfident and let herself indulge in a little emotional outing. And she ought to have known by now that there was no such thing as a *little* emotional outing. Given the slightest opportunity, emotions seemed wont to run absolutely amuck.

"I'm going home, Jackie. I'm going home just as soon as I . . . get my car checked out." Diana rocked back on her heels and tossed a handful of weeds on the little pile she'd made in the garden. She saw Jackie's head and back bobbing along above a low hedge of green beans. "Why did he have to tell me all that stuff about roots and his great-grandfather's sod house? The bottom line is, he's married. Why did I have to hear all that other stuff first?"

Jackie peered over the bean plants, the round lenses of her dark glasses glinting in the glare. "I don't know, Diana. I suppose he was trying to tell you why he thought Lori left him and . . . I don't know . . . why he thought you'd go back to Rhode Island, too. Maybe he didn't think he'd have to get to the bottom line. I'm sorry, Diana. I thought he'd gotten a divorce long ago."

"I believe you."

"When you think of it, he's really been away from her longer than you've been away from Doug. I mean, his being married is pretty much a technicality. One thing's for sure though—he'd never have that woman around again. I'll bet he'd gladly divorce her if he weren't worried about—"

"You were sure he *was* divorced," Diana reminded her friend, watching a ladybug settle on the red-veined leaf of the beet top nearest her nose. "So much for your knowing anything for sure."

"I don't like what he did, not telling you the whole truth. But give him a break. He loves Christopher, and he loves you, and now he's got to . . . Yike! Oh!" Jackie shot to her feet. "Oh," she sighed. "It was only a bull snake."

"Snake!" Diana scrambled to her feet in close imitation. "Where?"

"It's gone. Just a bull snake. We have to watch out, though. We get a rattlesnake in the yard once in a while."

Diana brushed indignantly at the dirt on her jeans. "You neglected to mention that little fact, old roomy. I'm out here risking my life for a pile of beets?"

"Once in a while, I said."

"That's once too often for me. How about if I use that hoe on these weeds? It looks nice and pointed."

A young voice interrupted them. "Diana!"

She searched for the caller and saw Christopher running toward the garden gate. Behind him, Brock's pickup was driving away. Diana's heart sank as she watched in the second before she caught herself and gave herself a mental kick. Stepping over beets and beans, she waved at the little boy and met him at the gate.

"We saw Jim out by the mailbox, and he said I should come and play with Jeff, and Daddy said I could. I told Daddy he should come and see you, but he said you might be busy. Are you?"

Diana let herself through the gate and lowered one knee to the ground beside Christopher. Smiling, she touched the Superman emblem on the front of his T-shirt. "No, I'm not busy, but I'm sure your daddy has work to do. I think the kids are in the barn with a batch of new kittens. Shall we go see?"

Christopher nodded vigorously.

The barn was cool and dim, a sudden change from the bright sunlight. It smelled of hay and horses, but no horses were there. The mewling of the kittens echoed in the corner of an empty stall, but no children were there, either. "They must've gone back out to play," Diana said, "but the kittens are here. Come on, let's take a peek."

She and Chris squatted in the straw beside the feed box that held a huge calico cat and her litter of five. "They're new babies," Diana whispered. "We'd better just look."

"Yeah. The mama might scratch us if we pick one up, huh?"

"She might."

"Where's their daddy?" Christopher asked.

"Probably catching mice for his family."

"The mama feeds the babies milk from her stomach. See?"

Diana nodded.

"Daddy says you're gonna leave pretty soon. Where are you going?"

"I have to go back to Rhode Island, where I live."

"How far away is that?"

"It's pretty far. It's by the ocean." Diana wondered how far he'd been from this spot and whether a number of miles would tell him anything.

"My mom left, too. I think she lives by the ocean. I don't think she's ever coming back, though. Is it fun to play in the ocean?"

"Yes, it's fun. It's fun to dig holes in the sand and watch the water fill them up."

"Like that story you told me?"

"Yes, like that story. Do you . . . remember your mother, Christopher?"

He thought a minute, then shook his head. "I don't think so. But I think she's pretty, but not as pretty as you. I asked Daddy, and he said you're a lot prettier."

Oh, Brock, have you coached this child? "Have you seen pictures of your mother?"

"No. Daddy says he doesn't have any." He watched the kittens for a moment, squatting there in an attentive little ball. Then he looked at her and said quietly, "I don't want you to go to Rhode Island, Diana, I want you to live here."

Diana took him in her arms, and he responded immediately with a hug. "Oh, sweetie, that's the nicest thing anyone's said to me in a very long time."

"If you'll stay, I'll find you lots of toads and frogs, and we can make houses."

"You have one very special frog, Christopher, but I don't think I have the magic to break his spell right now."

"Huh?"

Diana chuckled, rising to her feet with a bundle of little boy in her arms. "Nothing. Foolish talk. I wish I could stay, sweetheart, because I'd love to build frog houses all summer. You are one terrific little guy. Let's go find Jeff and Tracy and a few frogs or toads to play with right now."

For Christopher, Diana turned lunch into a party. She made up each child as a "grown-up" with Jackie's contributions of old clothes and hats. The big canvas duffel bag stuffed with outfits bound for Good Will yielded the makings of pirates and pretty ladies, with a shawl and a hat for Jackie and a full skirt to serve as a cape on Diana.

The fancy outfits were fine for a fancy party, but when

it came time to hunt big game, the dress-ups went back in the bag. Everyone got a jar. The quarry—the biggest toad in the yard.

Christopher spotted him first, lurking under the stem of a huge dahlia. First foot over the flower bed wall brought a warning from Jackie. "No, Christopher, you can't trample my flowers."

"I can't reach him. He's *really* big. Look, Diana!" Poor little Christopher was like the passenger on a merry-go-round who was too short to reach the ring.

"I can reach him," Diana said, bracing herself on the brick ledge. She braced herself, too, for the feeling of a handful of toad. "He is big, isn't he? Catch him over there if he hops away. Get ready now, Christopher, just in case I . . ."

She was concentrating on the toad, anticipating the direction of its inevitable hop. In the hedge behind, the rattler no doubt anticipated the same. When Diana's hand and the rattler's fangs converged at that spot beneath the pink dahlia, one lucky toad hopped away.

"Ohhh! My God! A snake!" Diana stared at the two red-welling pricks on the back of her hand. Finding her feet, she dragged Christopher back from the flower bed. "Jackie, I think . . . I think a rattlesnake . . ." She held the hand away from her, not sure whose it was. The pain was surely hers, but the hand had been bitten . . . by a poisonous snake! "Ahhh, it hurts." It was her own hand.

Diana's face puckered like a child's, reddened, and tears flowed quickly.

Jackie came running, screaming, "Where? Are you sure? Did you hear it rattle?"

Diana gestured to the flower bed, still pulling on Christopher's shoulder, towing him away. "Over there!" she shrieked. "Do you see it?"

Jackie leaned cautiously over tiptoeing feet. "Yes, there it . . ." She whirled back to her friend. "It *is* a rattler! Jim! Jim!"

Panic rose in her throat as Diana headed for the redwood deck, Christopher stumbling after the tether of her good hand. It was as though the injured hand led the way, a beacon held in front of her. Sometime in those moments Brock's pickup had pulled into the yard. Diana heard Jackie call out to him as she ran back from the barn, still looking for Jim.

I'd better sit down. Stay calm. Breathe quietly. There was a lawn chair under her, Diana realized, and she sank onto it. Then she watched the scene in the yard—Jackie's wild gesturing and Brock bursting from the pickup and running across the gravel. She had a fleeting image of Superman and a flying red cape.

"Daddy! A snake bit Diana!"

Stay calm. Stop crying. Mind over matter. Her hand lay on her lap, throbbing painfully, blood running down her fingers and dripping, one crimson drop at a time, past the inside of her thigh and into the webbing of the chair's seat.

"I can't find Jim." The high pitch of Jackie's voice echoed the brink of panic.

"He's out in the field. I just passed him. . . . Diana?"

"I'll stay with—no, I'll take her to . . . Brock, you take her to the—"

Brock lifted the hand from Diana's lap. "It's gonna be all right, Diana. I'll get you to a doctor quicker than you can . . . Does it hurt much?"

Her eyes were swimming. "Yes," she whispered, glancing at Christopher, who stood quietly beside her chair. She gave him what she hoped looked like a brave smile and then looked back up at Brock. "Please help me." She'd no more than got herself off the chair when Brock swept her into his arms.

"Jackie, get me a bucket of ice. Call the hospital and tell them we're coming. And call the police; tell them to send an escort. Chris, you stay with Jackie." Brock was on the other side of the backyard gate, striding toward the pickup. "Hurry with the ice," he called over his shoulder.

Diana lay on her stomach with her head in Brock's lap, her injured right hand dangling over the edge of the seat. She wanted to clutch it to her breast, to squeeze the pain away, but Brock told her that it must be kept below her head.

His voice flowed over her, telling her to lie still and breathe easily. Jackie brought a plastic pail of ice for her hand, and a moment later the pickup roared out of the yard. Brock kept talking to her in his deep, soothing voice, telling her they'd be there soon, telling her she'd be all right. His thigh flexed beneath her cheek when he pedaled the brake, and the road changed from gravel to blacktop.

"Have you ever known anyone who's been bitten?" Diana asked, putting real effort into sounding steady.

"Sure. One little kid, one old man, a dog, and a couple of cows. All of them came through it just fine. How do you feel?"

"Sick. Scared."

"Me, too."

"Aren't you going to cut an X in my hand and suck the poison out? Give me a story to tell . . . the eastern city slickers."

"Honey, I'm moving this outfit like a bat outta hell so I won't have to try any dramatic tricks. Here comes our escort." Brock flashed his headlights at the oncoming police car, which pulled over, reversed direction, and took the lead with flashing lights and whining siren. "We're gonna hit that emergency room in style, babe. That'll give you something to write home about." Lacing his fingers into the hair at Diana's temples, he found it wet from her tears. "I know you're hurting, honey. Hang on just a few more minutes. I wish I could—"

"I don't think I'll be . . . writing any letters for a while, not with this hand." She was striving for bravado, but the voice she heard herself producing sounded squeaky.

"I'll be your secretary."

Diana had a sense of losing touch with Brock, losing touch with the pickup, the road, the time of day. "Brock . . . please don't leave until . . . until Jackie comes. I'm so scared."

"I'll be there, hon. You can count on it."

Brock shouldered the wall next to the hospital bed. He stared at the bottle of water that hung from the tall stand, then let his eyes follow the narrow tubing from the bottle to the needle that was taped to Diana's arm. The terrible right hand was twice its normal size, something purple and green threatening to burst through the skin.

They kept telling him to go, but he kept ignoring them. She'd opened her eyes and looked at him several times, but she didn't seem to know him. He would stay until she knew he was there. He would stay until those murky eyes brightened and danced for him again.

A nurse and a blood pressure cuff meant a hospital, and a throbbing hand meant something, too. For the life of her, Diana couldn't figure it all out. Snakebite . . . the snake in the flower bed, and snatches of a ride, and wild dreams.

"My hand . . . my arm hurts."

"Your hand's still swollen, and your IV infiltrated, so we had to move it."

"I'm not going to die, am I?"

"Not today. You had a slight reaction to the antivenin, but that's all under control now, and you're out of the woods." The plump-faced woman smiled and pushed her glasses tight against the bridge of her nose. "Your friend Brock has made a real pest of himself around here. He's been determined to be the first person you'd recognize."

"Oh . . . don't let him see me like this . . . please."

"This is exactly how I want to see you. You've been trying to ignore me for what—two days now? Conversation's been pretty strange."

Diana cast a helpless look at the nurse as her left hand found the waxy mat of hair on the pillow. Nobody on TV woke up in the hospital looking like this. She heard the boots on the tile floor and turned her face to the sound. Brock approached the foot of her bed with a vase full of cut flowers—daisies and roses. His brown eyes sparkled.

"He's been in our way since you came in. We can't seem to get rid of him for more than an hour at a time," the nurse explained with a shrug. "He doesn't eat or sleep much. Easy keeper, as they say. He's your problem now." She winked at Brock as she glided out the door.

"These are from Mom," Brock said, setting the vase on the bed table. "And this"—a brown paper sack was brandished in front of her nose—"is from Christopher." He slid out a jar and held it for her inspection. A toad. "I promised. He says it's the one that got away." The jar disappeared into the sack.

"Tell him to keep it for me." Diana attempted a smile, and Brock nodded.

"How do you feel?"

"I'm not sure. I think I hurt in a few places. But it would seem that you got me here in time, and I'm grateful."

Coming to the bedside, Brock brushed a lock of dark hair back from his forehead. "I heard that if it hadn't been you, it would have been Christopher. Either way . . ." He sat on the side of the bed, covering her good hand with his. "Either way, I was in for a hell of a scare."

"I can't claim any credit for . . . I didn't know Christopher was in danger. But thank God it wasn't him. He's so little."

He ached to hold her, but he only smiled and said, "If there'd been a choice, I'd have taken it myself. I'm bigger than both of you." He was quiet for a moment, looking at their hands. "I don't want to lose you, Diana."

They looked at one another, willing understanding. "You know . . . how much of me . . ." She swallowed hard and glanced away. "You have."

"Not enough. Never enough."

"I'll leave here loving you. There's no help for it." Another quiet moment passed. "So you see, it's going to turn out the way you thought it would. A short, sweet little love story—sad, but not tragic—the principals going on with their lives as before."

"You won't be leaving for a while now, and I won't be able to stay away from you. You know that." He touched her pale cheek, his thumb at her chin.

Her eyes closed briefly. "We're at sad but sweet right now, Brock. If we go on seeing each other, things could get bitter. I don't want that."

"You don't want to see me?" he asked quietly.

The word wouldn't come. "Thank you for being here through this. Now I think—"

"I had to be here, Diana. Where else would I be? I had

to give you this.'' He dipped his head and planted a soft kiss on her mouth. "This is from me," he muttered against her lips, and kissed her again.

A moment later he was gone, and Diana felt the tears slipping along her temples and into her hair.

Chapter Eleven

The swelling in Diana's hand subsided slowly. Within a week she was able to return to the Reinharts'. She immediately began to think about driving home. Jackie insisted it was out of the question until she was certain of Diana's good health. The wound was lightly bandaged with gauze and had to be kept perfectly clean. Tired as Diana was, it wasn't difficult to persuade her to take it easy.

She stayed out of the yard and out of the garden. The deck looked fairly safe, but she made a habit of looking for hidden vipers before she sat out there. The sun was beginning to drop toward the horizon one evening when she walked onto the deck, sliding the glass door closed behind her, effectively shutting off the sound of an argument between Tracy and Jeff. Diana had thought to give the family some privacy, and she took her after-dinner sherry to this place, where she could indulge her mood.

Anyone watching would laugh at her reconnaissance with a long stick under the chairs and benches. Anyone watching probably hadn't suffered from snakebite. Diana leaned both elbows on the redwood railing and held the burnished shimmer in a glass between both hands. The skyline here was hard and angular, the hills squared off into buttes. No trees to speak of. Only the sky softened the land with its color. This was her second glass of sherry, and she felt like marching up the side of a butte to get a closer look at that watercolor sky. But that was probably where the snakes lived.

The familiar blue-and-silver pickup churned up its wake of dust and gravel as it charged Diana's lookout point. There was no sense in ducking into the house. She'd hold her ground, possibly wave as he drove by. He hadn't tried to see her since he'd left his flowers and his kiss at the hospital. The pickup drew closer. If he stopped, she'd tell him he shouldn't stay. But if he drove by, her heart would plummet.

He stopped. Diana waited, watching him spring from the cab, swing the door shut, and stride around the front of the vehicle, gravel crunching under his boots. She'd wait for his greeting, or his words of concern, or his I-was-just-passing-by excuse. She'd lean against the railing, too nonchalant to speak until he spoke first.

Brock bypassed the gate, walked up to the deck railing, took Diana's shoulders in his hands, and lifted her into his kiss. He took her breath away.

"Let's go for a drive," he said, smiling at the kiss-softened, speechless lips.

"Where?"

"It doesn't matter. If we hurry, we can find a nice, quiet spot and watch the sun set and the stars come out." He took the glass from her hand. "You finished with this?" She nodded dumbly, and he drained the last of it himself, leaned over to set the glass on the table, and pressed his lips together. "Sweet." Then he nodded toward the pickup.

Diana sighed as she let herself through the waist-high redwood gate. She shouldn't feel this desperate need to see him again. But she did, and she was too old to play cat-and-mouse. The door to the pickup opened, and she hopped from the running board onto the seat.

"I sort of thought we realized that not seeing each other would be best for both of us," she said as Brock swung into a gravel road she'd not been on before.

"Obviously neither of us is convinced. When I saw you standing out there on the deck, there was no chance of driving by."

"How could you tell from the road who was standing there?"

"I knew."

Diana looked at him for a moment—his denim jacket, pale yellow shirt, straw cowboy hat, jeans—a strange image for the one man in her life who could steal her sensibilities and make her do the very thing she'd sworn not to do. She turned her attention to the road ahead, the steep little butte not far in front of them. "Ever climb a butte?" she asked.

He grinned. "I was about to ask you that."

"I read your mind. Up there looks like a terrific vantage point for sky watching."

The pickup surged ahead under Brock's heavy foot. Wind from the open window whipped Diana's hair across her face, and she tossed it back again. "Let's see if we can beat the sun," Brock said. He cast his hat on the seat between them and leaned his head out the window. "Yee-hah! I'm gainin' on you, sun!"

The wind straightened his curls, and when he ducked

back in his hair was wind wild, his laughter that of a carefree teenager racing his dad's pickup along a country road.

"The police'll cut this outing short if you don't slow down," Diana shouted over the roar of the wind and the engine.

"Relax, Prudence, this is *my* road. And that's *my* butte, and up there's *my* sky, and I'm gonna share the whole works with *my* girl. Ain't *no*body gonna cut this outing short."

They left the road and then left the pickup, Brock taking along the extra denim jacket he had stashed behind the seat, and they hiked to the top of the little hill.

"Look at that!" Brock gestured toward the horizon where the sun still hovered over the earth's margin. "We beat him. Look, Diana. There's my place, and over there's the Reinharts'." His hand was on the back of her neck, and he pointed over her shoulder at the distant little buildings, the patches of ground that varied in color in this light from tan to gold to yellow-green. "Isn't this a great spot? You can see for miles. And look at that horizon," he marveled. "Somebody took a purple crayon and drew a jagged line under the sky."

"Then he brushed that blue sky with streaks of pink and orange. It isn't your charm that I find so seductive, you know," Diana told him. "It's the colors and the bright lights in this huge sky of yours."

He shrugged boyishly, the breeze ruffling his hair again, and the flash of white teeth in his wide grin coaxed a bright smile from Diana. "Some guys use pretty words; some flash their money around. Me—I just got the sun in the mornin' and the moon at night."

"Seems to do the trick with me. You know, you look

like a seventeen-year-old kid tonight." She couldn't resist touching the dark wave that fell across his forehead.

"And you hardly look the lady lawyer in your blue jeans and tennis shoes."

"Just for one evening, let's be kids. No problems, no pasts—just two young lovers who managed to slip away from everyone and be alone for a little while."

He dropped the extra jacket on the tall grass before he turned her toward the west, toward the setting sun, and he stood behind her, his arms encircling her shoulders and his mouth near her ear.

The sun was slipping into its bedsack, leaving its paths of fire colors behind. They stood quietly for a moment, the breeze bathing their faces in summer evening. He turned her to him and pushed his fingers through her flaxen, windblown hair. "I never wanted to hurt you, Prudence. You know that."

Her eyes suddenly bristled, reality insinuating itself in her brain. "But you did."

"I know. But I couldn't help loving you. If you don't believe anything else, believe that I never wanted to hurt you. I've given you everything I have to give, and, God help me, one day I'll—"

"Not tonight, Brock." She touched the corner of his mouth with her injured hand. "Let's say those things another time. Tonight there are no complications."

He smiled and brought the bandaged palm to his lips. "How's your hand?"

"I'd forgotten. You don't suppose there are any rattlesnakes up here, do you?"

"Rattlesnakes? You got hurt . . . cheerleading, wasn't it? I came crashing down on you when I was shoved out-of-bounds, remember?"

"And I'll wear the scars from your spikes with pride."

"I gained fifteen yards on that play."

"It was worth it, too. We won the game."

He nuzzled her temple and whispered, "Let me make it all up to you somehow. Maybe we could just . . . fool around a little?"

With a smile she put her arms around him and slipped her hands under the denim jacket. His mouth came looking for the good taste of hers. Once again she gave him sweet sherry, this time from her own tongue. Diana heard the quick intake of his breath and felt his chest expand, just as hers did when she inhaled the smell of him, the full sense of him, filling her mouth, her lungs, her arms.

He spread the fingers of one hand over her back and with the other bridged the back pockets of her jeans as he pulled her flush against him. She moaned, overwhelmed by his masculinity, admitting an age-old feminine weakness. She wanted to damn the circumstances and give him the full measure of a woman's trust.

He cupped her cheek in his palm as he drew his mouth back from hers, smiling past the desire that burned in his eyes. "Will you lie here in the grass with me?"

"Only a toad would bed his lady in the grass," she teased, her voice husky.

He shrugged out of his jacket. "Who was that noble cavalier who spread his cloak on the ground for the lady to walk on?" Dropping one knee in the grass, he spread their jackets on the ground.

"Sir Walter Raleigh?"

"That's the one. The model toad." He sat beside the jackets and extended a hand to her. "Just let me hold you a while."

She knelt beside him, and he took her in his arms,

easing her down on the bed he'd made. He meant to show her the purity of his love with a tender kiss. But her breath was warm against his cheek, and her breasts were soft beneath his chest. He knew how sweet they tasted. His body hardened at the thought, his kiss deepened, and his tongue sought hers. He pressed the heel of his hand against the side of her breast, and he heard the catch in her breath. She wanted him the same way he wanted her, and something wild inside him said *Love her more*.

He slid his hand over her stomach and caressed her through her jeans. "I want you to have another baby, Diana," he whispered. "I want it to be mine."

"Brock . . ."

"You'd let me put our baby here, wouldn't you? If we were married?"

"Yes. Yes, I'd want that very much."

"I'd never insist. I'd be happy just to have you."

"I know. But I . . . Oh, God, Brock, don't talk about things that can't—"

"You'll have my baby someday, Diana. Right here, in this little cradle." He kissed her as he unsnapped her jeans, but she covered his hand with hers before he could find the zipper. He lifted his head and looked at her. "Let me make love with you."

"It won't work for me now." Her quick, shallow breathing proved that she had no trouble responding physically.

"Nothing's changed, Diana. I'm still—"

"Nothing's changed for you," she whispered, struggling against the tears rising in her throat. "For me it has."

"Do you love me, Diana?" He slid his hand to her breast again, and his eyes burned bright with a need

beyond the physical. "Do you love me?" Her brief nod
was not enough. "Say it."

"I love you, Brock. That hasn't changed." He closed
his eyes and allowed himself to breathe. "What's changed
is that I know you're not truly free. I believe in marriage,
and it would be wrong . . . wrong for *me* . . ."

Her tears stung him. He pulled her into his arms, lay
back in the grass, and held her. "I'm not wrong for you,"
he insisted, talking as much to himself as to her. "I was
wrong to keep the truth from you, but I wasn't wrong to
love you. Nothing's ever been so right for me as you are."

"Right girl, wrong time." She took two slow, deep
breaths and stemmed the tears. "Got a handkerchief?"

"You're welcome to the front of my shirt, or the shirt
off my back, or anything else—" She managed a sad little
laugh as she brushed at her tears with the back of her
hand, and his heart lightened at the sound. "The right
girl," he said as he rubbed her back. "The kind of girl
who tells a guy to keep his hands to himself no matter how
many touchdowns he made."

"Every game has its rules," she whispered.

"I just need some time, Diana. I know that sounds like
some kind of feeble—"

"Brock, please." She lifted her head and covered his
lips with the tips of her fingers. "We know where we
stand. Let's put it aside and talk about stars, sports, Shake-
separe, anything but sex—"

"Snakes?"

"Anything but sex and snakes," she amended as she
turned over on her back and pillowed her head against his
shoulder.

"Anything but how good it feels to hold you."

"Mmm. Anything but the way the sound of your heart beating right next to my ear makes me . . ."

"Me, too," he whispered as he nestled his chin in her hair. He allowed several silent moments to pass, then cleared his throat. "Heard any good star stories lately?"

"No, but this big, bas—bullheaded farmer told me a bunch of Shakespeare jokes."

He chuckled and stroked her arm. "Rancher."

Diana planned to take the drive home in leisurely fashion, allowing a day longer than it had taken her to drive west. Jackie slouched on the chair in the bedroom, watching each freshly laundered item go into the suitcase on the bed and grumbling that Diana shouldn't leave yet. Diana knew that her friend would never willingly let her go. Jackie was a nester, and mentally she'd already adopted Diana, tucked her under a full-feathered wing.

The only way to make this break was quickly and quietly. No farewells, no plans or promises. With some extra care she folded her western-style skirt and blouse and smiled as she settled them in the suitcase.

"Fond memories?" Jackie asked.

"What do you mean?"

"I caught that look on your face in the mirror, old friend."

"Yes, fond memories. I'm taking those with me."

"And some regrets?"

"Yes. One. Our timing was off. Maybe if we'd met sooner . . . or later . . ."

"Oh, hogwash." Jackie expelled the word like a prune pit. "What happened to the good old take-charge Diana? You always made things work out. You always—"

"I always got what I wanted. But once I had it, it didn't always turn out to be satisfying." Diana sighed and sat on the bed, facing Jackie's frown with the patient, open-handed gesture of one who was about to explain something very complex. "I married a man I'd groomed for the job of mating with me, and that's about what we did. We looked good together, bought the right things, came together physically on a regularly scheduled basis, and wondered why we didn't make each other happy. The world came crashing down when Robbie died. There was nothing between Doug and me to get us through that. We never touched.

"Now I'm in love with a man, but I didn't prepare him for his role. I forgot to make sure his life was in order. I forgot to mention that he would not be permitted to lie to me. I forgot to lay down the rules and set the schedule. Sure enough, things got all screwed up, just as I knew they would if I lost control. But you know what? I love him anyway. What he did, he did out of self-defense, which he's even better at than I am."

Jackie sat up and leaned forward in her chair. "Don't you think you can work things out?"

"There's nothing to work out. Brock's afraid to make any waves, and who knows? Lori might actually be lurking out there somewhere, ready to pounce."

"But you're a lawyer. You could help him with that."

Diana shook her head. "I offered. That's all I can do. He isn't ready."

Both women jumped at the sound of the slamming back door. "Diana!"

Jackie's hand went to her mouth as Diana turned to her, eyes wide. "I'm sorry," Jackie whispered. "I guess I let it slip over the phone."

"He called?"

"Diana!" Brock roared again, getting closer.

"Um, no . . . I called him a little while ago."

"Jackie! You *knew* I didn't want—"

"Well, you ought to say good-bye, at least." Jackie was on her feet and edging away, as though expecting a lash. "I know, I know. I meddled. I shouldn't have."

Brock appeared in the doorway, dressed for the day's work in jeans and a faded blue shirt, his straw cowboy hat still perched on his head. He said nothing, but his eyes darted some accusations in Diana's direction.

"I'll just . . . leave you two alone," Jackie muttered, scooting past him.

He took two steps toward the bed, and then, at the look in her eyes, the expression in his face softened a bit. "You were just going to leave . . . without a word?" he asked quietly.

"You knew I'd be leaving soon. I thought it would be best just to make a . . . a clean getaway, as they say." Her attempt at a little laugh failed miserably.

"Best for what?"

"The best way to end the story. 'She was not the real princess, so she disappeared and was not heard from again.' "

With one swift movement he lifted her by the shoulders and shook her to clear the static in her head. "Look at me."

She resisted.

"Look at me, Diana. Do I look like a fairy-tale prince? I'm a flesh-and-blood man, dammit, a working man, plain and simple. And I'm in love with a flesh-and-blood woman who's about to leave me because I'm tied up legally with a woman I want no part of. Don't try to brush me off with some cute remark.''

"What do you want, Brock? Tears? I can give you plenty of those, but they won't change anything. I've asked you to . . . to free yourself, but you aren't ready for that. I don't want to leave here with a carload of promises, and I'd hoped to avoid any angry scenes between us. I could get angry, you know. I could get very angry all over again for the way you—''

"Lied to you . . . I know. I don't feel good about that. I know that wasn't fair, but that's got to be water under the bridge now.''

Too close. He stood too close, smelling of citrusy green soap and spicy shaving cream and Brock. She clutched his wrists and pulled his hands down her arms until he released her. "It is, Brock. It's water under the bridge.'' Turning from him gave her time to regroup. "Last night was the perfect ending for us. It was something just for us, a time removed from everything else. Now . . .'' She turned to face him again, blinking back the threat of tears. "Now I have to go, before we muddy things up with more words. There *are* no more words.''

"You don't just slip out of a man's life like this, Diana, not if you love him. You don't sneak away like some . . .''

She glanced down at clenched fists and up into eyes dark with hurt. "I am not sneaking away,'' she said calmly. "You know where I'm going; you know where I'll be. Brock . . . there's no place for me in your life. You say you love me, but that isn't enough. There has to be a place for me.'' She sighed, shrugging helplessly. "Anyway, if we go on with this conversation, pretty soon I'll start the 'if you really loved me' routine.''

He stared through her, and Diana wondered what he

saw. A few moments ago she could have sworn that if anyone had been wronged here, it had been she. "I'm trying to retire my side gracefully, Brock. I'm not sneaking away, although I do feel somewhat defeated. I've always been very pragmatic, but I guess this time I had my cap set for happily ever after."

"Maybe there still could've been, but not like this. . . ."

What was he talking about? Diana flopped her arms before him, another helpless grunt accompanying the gesture. "Don't you see? We have too many problems to just kiss away, and problem number one is that you're *married*."

"Not if you're just going to leave without a word. . . ."

He was completely exasperating. "Well, let me tell you," she said evenly, "there must be at least a hundred ways to leave your lover, but I'm pointing that car in an easterly direction and headin' for the dock, Brock."

It was a momentary stare-down. Then he summoned new direction from somewhere inside himself, and a detached voice said, "Christopher wants to see you before you go. He's outside; I'll send him in. I'd appreciate it if you'd remember how he feels about you."

He'd reached the doorway when Diana found her own voice. "To be fair, you might consider how I feel about him. I love him . . . as though he were my own."

Brock stood in the doorway for just a moment, and then, without turning, he said, "I know you do. Have a safe trip."

Seeing little Christopher, Diana renewed her battle against the tears. He went into her arms, and she dragged him onto her lap, squeezing her eyes shut as she hugged him.

"Daddy says you're going away."

"I have to get back to my job and my apartment," she

explained, loosening her hold on him. "I've been gone a long time."

"I thought you were gonna stay here . . . with Daddy and me," he pouted, taking the polished stone beads she wore in one fat little hand and bringing them close to his face. "Are these made out of marbles?"

Diana smiled. "No . . . well, they're sort of like marbles. They're all kinds of rocks, polished and made into round beads."

"Did you get them at the ocean?"

"At a store near the ocean. But the ocean didn't make them like this."

"The river makes rocks smooth like this. I have a whole bunch of rocks like this, but not so shiny. I could tie 'em together and make a necklace for you," he offered hopefully. His voice fell. "But it wouldn't be so pretty."

She hugged him again. "If you made it, it would be beautiful, and I'd wear it with my very best dress."

"You could come over to my house and see them," he suggested, his brown eyes wide with anticipation.

"No, sweetheart, I can't."

"We have two beds that nobody sleeps in. You could have your own room at our house." Taking a breath, Christopher launched a quick-tongued sales pitch. "Daddy would like that a lot because he likes you a whole lot—he said he does. And I'd be real good. You wouldn't have to take care of me much. I'll be in kindergarten a lot. And if you cooked carrots or beans, I'd just eat 'em and wouldn't say a word—"

"Oh, Christopher . . . Christopher." Diana nodded, eyes closed against those irritating tears. "You are a good boy. I want you to know that I love you very much." She brushed his unruly curls back from his face. "Did you know that I had a little boy of my own?'' Christopher shook his head. ''I did. A baby boy. I lost him a couple of years ago when—''

''Did he get lost in the mall?''

''No, Christopher, he died. And I was very sad for a very long time. But you . . . you've made me happy again because knowing you has been like—''

''What was your little boy's name?''

''Robbie.''

''I could be your little boy *and* Daddy's boy. My mama isn't coming back, so I bet I *could* be. My name would still be Christopher, but you could call me—''

''Christopher. I want you to be Christopher. Will you always be my Christopher, no matter where you are and no matter where I am?''

Christopher nodded.

Diana held him against her. ''I'm going to show you the ocean someday. That's a promise.''

Chapter Twelve

"Diana, where were you at Thanksgiving? We called several times." Jackie's voice always had that note of motherly indignation when she was concerned.

"Orlando with my mother. You should see me now. I'll be brown almost 'til Christmas. How's your weather?"

"Two feet of snow on the ground. Listen, I'm worried about Brock. We hardly ever see him. *Nobody* ever sees him."

"He's not sick or anything, is he?"

"Well, no, he left Christopher here to play with the kids today. But he never visits. When he comes in, he hardly says anything. Have you talked to him, heard from him at all?"

"No. He's probably quite busy. I imagine he has a lot to do, especially if the weather's been bad. Is Christopher there now? I'd like to say hello." Diana waited while the receiver changed hands. "Hello, Christopher? How are you, sweetheart? This is Diana."

"Diana? Guess what! I'm in kindergarten now. I have a teacher named Miss Baker who looks kinda like you, but not really. She doesn't like frogs much. I brought one to show the class, but she wouldn't pick it up herself. But we made a place for it in a glass box with sand in it and water and a rock. No little house, though. When are you coming back?''

Diana laughed, swallowing the lump in her throat. ''I don't know, honey. I took such a long vacation last summer, so it might be—''

''There's Christmas vacation pretty soon. How 'bout Christmas vacation?''

''I only have a short time at Christmas, honey. How's Jake?''

''He's fine.''

''And how's your daddy?''

''He's fine, too. I get to ride a big yellow bus to school. Lots of times Daddy picks me up after school, though. Lots of times he has business in town. That's okay, though, because it's longer riding the bus.''

''Your daddy does lots of business in town?''

''Yeah, lots of days. When can I come and see the ocean?''

''The ocean gets cold and angry in the winter. We'll wait 'til summer, when it's warm and sleepy and just right for swimming. I miss you, sweetheart. You draw me some pictures in school and send them to me, okay?''

''Do you have any pictures of me? I had my picture taken in school, and I asked Daddy if I could give you one, and he said I could.''

''I'd love that.''

''And I'll draw pictures of Daddy and Jake and me and you, okay? I have a new box of colors. My other ones got broken. I let Jason Skyler share, and he presses too hard.''

"I'll bet he does. You send me those pictures, and I'll send something special for you."

Diana had found just the Christmas gift for Christopher —an apartment house for a hamster, complete with see-through plastic hallways and rooms. She knew he'd love it, and she knew Brock would grudgingly go along with another pet. But she wanted Christopher to have something of herself, and, remembering the appliqué quilt she'd made for Robbie, she designed one especially for her frog-loving friend. Each square was a scene from "Frog Went a-Courtin'," and she'd worked steadily on it most nights during the fall months while she listened to music or watched TV.

She was doing some handwork on Miss Mousey's wedding dress when the phone rang one evening. She answered with a distracted "Hello?"

"I woke up this morning wanting you so bad I was shaking."

Diana's dry throat allowed only a croak. "Brock?"

"Has anyone else been in a position to tell you that lately?"

"No." Her heart skittered against her ribs at the very sound of his voice.

"I love you. Has anyone else told you that lately?"

"No."

"That's all? Just 'no'?"

"Um . . . I guess I'm surprised you know how to dial long distance. How are you?"

"I told you. I'm in a pretty bad way. I miss you."

She hadn't realized how much she'd wanted to hear him say that. "Other than that, how are you? I talked to Christopher a couple of weeks ago. He sounds—"

"We're both well, Diana, but we're both lonely. He talked about nothing but you for days afterward."

"I'm sorry. Maybe I shouldn't have talked to him, but I wanted to . . . hear his voice."

"How does my voice sound to you?"

"It sounds . . . it's good to hear your . . . Oh, God . . ."

"What's wrong, Diana?"

She took a deep breath, steadying herself. "It's just really good to hear from you, that's all. Tell me what you did today and yesterday and the day before. Just talk. Just let me hear your—"

"Diana, I'm sorry I haven't called or anything. I just didn't want to butt into your life until I could . . . Would you be willing to see me?"

"See you?"

"I mean, if I showed up at your door, would you let me in?"

"Of course I'd—"

"That's all I wanted to know. I'll be seeing you, then." The phone clicked and buzzed.

Diana held the receiver away and looked at it as though it had done something strange. Then she dropped it back on the cradle with a sigh. The room that had warmed for a moment seemed chilly again. It was the high ceiling, just ate up the heat. Put another log on the fire, put on a tape, finish reading the Cleary brief, and then finish Miss Mousey's dress, she told herself.

The fire, framed by the marble firebox, leaped away from the point of the bellows as though it had been pinched. Sparks floated toward the flue as Diana replaced the screen. She chose a tape, tucked it into the slot on the machine, and pressed "play" just as the knock sounded on the door. She looked down at herself. Her long jade-and-gold brocade kimono. She'd felt like being sumptuous tonight.

"Who is it?" she called through the door.

"Ribit."

Oh, my God. "Brock?"

"I should be hibernating. Too damn cold out here for us . . ."

The deadbolt lock wouldn't cooperate with her fingers fast enough, but she got it on the second try.

"Frogs." He wore a sheepskin coat with the sheepish grin on his face, a russet cowboy hat in his hands, looking for all of Newport like a young McCloud.

"Brock!" It was Diana who leaped, and Brock caught her off the floor. He stepped across the threshold, carrying her with him. "Brock, what are you doing here?" She leaned back to get another look at her surprise guest. "You just called . . . I thought from . . ."

"From down the street at that pay phone. God, you look beautiful." He pulled her back into his arms and leaned down to kiss her, intending it to be a gentle greeting but finding that a thirsty man needed more than just a sip of water. When at last he was able to take a breath, he took the time to fill his eyes with the image that had haunted him for months.

"You really caught me by surprise." Diana's fingers found the planes of his cheek and the thickness of his hair, recognizing him by touch as a blind person would. "I almost thought you'd forgotten."

"Forgotten? Forgotten what? The way your hair smells like lemons and dips over your right eyebrow?" His long fingers touched that wave, rubbed it between them. "The way the gold dust dances in your eyes when you look up at me and smile just after I've kissed you? The way your long back tightens into a V just above your heart-shaped little bottom?'' His hand traced the path over the loose-fitting brocade. ''I haven't forgotten a thing.''

''I should ask you whatever possessed you to—''

''You possessed me. You've possessed my mind since the day you left, so I figured you might want to possess my body again.''

''When did you decide?''

''I told you. This morning.''

''What if I'd said I wouldn't see you?''

''I'd have taken the next plane back to Bismarck.''

She laughed, delighted just to see his face. ''I doubt that.''

''I do, too. I had to see you. God, I don't believe how great you look. You've been sunworshiping again.''

''Let me take your coat and hat,'' she offered, unfastening the big buttons to expedite her suggestion.

''I can just drop them on the floor with the rest of my clothes.'' Grinning, he watched her as she moved around him, and he lowered his shoulders to let the heavy coat slide off his back into her hands.

''Do you have luggage?'' She pulled a wooden hanger from the closet.

''Very little.'' Reaching outside the door, he retrieved a small brown carry-on bag. He closed the door, setting the bag just inside. ''What is this, some old mansion?'' he asked, looking up at the high ceiling and then down to the polished wood floor.

Diana nodded. ''Remodeled into apartments. Newport is where I grew up, but I work in Providence. When we sold the house in Providence, I decided to come back here. I love these old homes. Your house has this kind of homey feeling. Come sit by the fire with me. Would you like a glass of . . . sherry is all I have. Oh, no, I think I have some drier white wine.''

"I'll take the dry stuff." Brock followed her, his boot heels clomping across the floorboards. The kitchen was long and narrow but with modern equipment and plenty of fluorescent lighting.

"This was the butler's pantry," Diana explained, reaching for glasses. When her arms hiked the kimono up a bit, Brock glimpsed her bare legs and smiled, remembering.

"What are your plans for Christmas?"

"Oh, I'll probably have dinner with friends."

"Where's your tree?" he asked, accepting the corkscrew and the wine bottle from her. .

"I'll get one. I've still got almost two weeks."

"We haven't put one up yet, either. Christopher wanted to wait for . . ."

She waited. "For what?"

"Oh, he thinks he has to have this special present to put under it. Something he thinks we both need." Brock shrugged, laying the corkscrew on the counter as he poured the wine. "I told him I'd try to get it by Christmas. That's one of the toughest things about being a parent. No matter what the kid wants for Christmas, you feel like you have to try to come up with it."

"And what's this thing you both need?"

He handed her a glass. "You." Tasting the wine, he said, "Not bad. Here." He fished a small picture from his breast pocket. "This is something I promised to deliver, along with a pile of pictures he colored for you."

Diana smiled fondly at the dark-haired moppet, who smiled back up at her from the picture. On the back he'd printed his name in a novice hand. "I have some things I'd like you to take back for him."

"Let's get those bare feet by the fire."

The sofa was big and overstuffed, sculptured blue velour upholstery. Brock took one end, setting his glass on the side table, and Diana took the other, curling her feet underneath her.

"You look like a big, beautiful green bird perched on the edge of the sofa. Are you going to fly if I reach for you?"

Diana closed her eyes and listened to her heart pound. "Reach for me, Brock. But this time, don't let me go." She felt her shoulders corraled by two large hands. Eyes open, she tumbled into the depths of his gaze.

"I couldn't call you before this, Diana. I had no right to intrude in your life again until I put my house in order. Now . . . now I can reach for you and hold you, touch you without feeling so damned guilty."

Diana blinked, afraid to ask what that meant.

"I looked for her," he explained. "I wanted to have it all out on the table—all the cards, all plays, all bets. I've seen the elephant, as they say."

"And?"

"And Lori is nowhere to be found. Her parents are dead; no one else knows anything about her. I even hired a private investigator. The last man she was with had . . . questionable connections. She could well be dead. The divorce was just a matter of filing some papers."

"How do you feel about her now?"

He shook his head. "I should've done it long ago. I don't feel anything about her—haven't for a long time. It was always Christopher. I was afraid of any risks where he was concerned. I was paralyzed by that fear."

"I know," she said. "I know that kind of fear."

"But I didn't want to lose you, either. And Chris has

asked every day of every week when you were coming back. Stubborn little kid. He thinks anybody who doesn't have a mother oughta be able to pick one out for himself. He misses you." The loneliness was etched in Brock's own eyes, and Diana knew before he said it. "Come back with me, Diana. Marry me."

"You just want to play Santa Claus."

"I wanna play house. It's Christopher who wants to play Santa Claus. He'd have come to get you himself. He thinks you're . . . it's a vacant spot in his life. He's never had a mother. I've never had a wife."

Diana cocked her head to one side, smiling, touching his square chin with two fingers. "And I've never had a real lover. Of all the ways to go back to him, marriage appeals to me the most."

Brock laughed, taking the glass of wine from her hand. "When you came up with that line about 'heading for the dock, Brock,' I saw red."

"I guess that was a bit flip."

"No, it was pretty damn cute. I was mad because I couldn't top it. And I was mad at you for being right— there was no way for us to go on seeing each other until I cleared the skeletons out on my side of the closet."

Reaching over the arm of the sofa to set her glass beside his, he noticed the quilt square in the embroidery hoop on the table. "What's this? Are you making something?" He picked up the hoop, an incongruity in his big hand. "You don't seem the embroidery type."

"What type is that? The mousey type?" She drew a sideways glance and a chuckle from him as she slid closer on the seat. "That's Miss Mousey. She and I have nothing in common except a penchant for frogs. I enjoy needle-work. Look, I'm almost finished." Retrieving her sewing basket from under the table, she knelt on the floor with a stack of appliquéd quilt squares, singing each scene as she laid it over his thigh. "It's for Christopher's bed," she explained, excitement evident in her voice. "Will he like it?"

"He'll love it. And you, clever lady, must have known I'd be along sooner or later."

"Why? Because I made this? This isn't for you; it's for Christopher. He's special to me, and not because he's your son. Christopher and I have our very own thing going. We love each other, too, in case you hadn't noticed."

"I noticed. And I notice you and Miss Mousey do have similar taste in suitors. Come on, Miss Diana, sit on ol' Froggie's knee and let's plan our own wedding." Eyes twinkling, Brock patted his knee with one hand and offered the other to pull her up from the floor.

Cuddling against his chest, she asked, "Can we do it soon?"

"How about Christmas? Christmas Eve."

"Lovely idea," she said, fingering the pearl snap on his shirt.

"What about your job?"

"I'll have to come back after Christmas and get everything sorted out. I'll admit to having given a great deal of thought to this in the form of 'what if' propositions."

"What if that half-wit cowboy ever comes to his senses?"

"Something like that. I'll have to do some studying for another bar exam, won't I?" She released one snap on his shirt and smiled up at him.

"Mmm-hmm. I'll even help you study. Now where's the master bedroom in this place?"

Diana flicked open a second snap and felt him rub his chin against the top of her head. "This is it."

"You're kidding. I suppose your underwear is all over the floor in your bedroom."

"No, this is it." She slid from his lap, and his eyes followed her to an alcove across the room. She unfastened some hardware on what looked like a big, hardwood-paneled door, and presto! A bed appeared out of the wall.

"What the hell," Brock said, coming lazily to his feet. "I saw one of those in a movie once. The guy pressed the wrong button and got shut back up in the wall."

"That's right." Diana turned off the wall light, leaving the room shadowed, firelight favoring the shapes of things with flickering illumination. "And if your performance tonight doesn't please me perfectly, I need only press a button, and poof!" She had sauntered up to him and snapped her fingers in his face. "You become, quite literally, a stud."

His fingers found the cloth fastenings of her kimono, but while she made short work of all snaps, he was stymied. "I'm not off to a good start, honey. How do you work these crazy things?"

Her smaller fingers had no trouble with them. "They're frogs." She giggled, and he rolled his eyes. "Really, that's what they're called. Frogs."

"Oh, geez. I swear to God, Diana, I can't even swim worth a damn." Her robe was open now, and he backed her the few steps into the alcove before he pushed the sumptuous brocade off her shoulders and let it drop to the floor. Her body glimmered firelight gold. He breathed a kiss on the curve of her shoulder. "Tell you what I can do, though. I can hop from here . . ." His lips fell on the swell of her breast. "Down to here . . ." Darting tongue teased a taut nipple. "And make you shiver. Remember?"

"Mmm."

"Remember . . . how you quiver all over for me?"

Her head dropped back as his touch caused a fluttering in the pit of her stomach. "Yes, Brock," she whispered, "I do remember."

After the loving, after they'd said "I love you" in every conceivable way and they lay in each other's arms watching the waning fire, Brock cracked the contented silence with a chuckle.

"What's so funny?"

"How in hell could a mouse and a frog get married? What kinds of kids would they have?"

"I don't know. Jacktoads. Long, green, hairy back legs, short ears, pointy noses."

"What a mess. You can only go so far with crossbreeding," Brock declared seriously. "I think we've got a crisis here. No matter how many times you kiss me, a toad is still a toad."

"Maybe we've been going about it all wrong. What if the toad kisses the princess? Come on, let's give it a try—for happily-ever-after's sake."

It was a most compatible kiss.

"Well?" he murmured.

Restless embers stirred in the quiet. Diana snuggled her mouth near Brock's ear. "Ribit."

The End?

The end of a book is never really *the end* for a person who reads. He or she can always open another. And another.

Every page holds possibilities.

But millions of kids don't see them. Don't know they're there. Millions of kids can't read, or won't.

That's why there's RIF. Reading is Fundamental (RIF) is a national nonprofit program that works with thousands of community organizations to help young people discover the fun—and the importance—of reading.

RIF motivates kids so that they *want* to read. And RIF works directly with parents to help them encourage their children's reading. RIF gets books to children and children into books, so they grow up reading and become adults who can read. Adults like you.

For more information on how to start a RIF program in your neighborhood, or help your own child grow up reading, write to:

RIF
Dept. BK-1
Box 23444
Washington, D.C.
20026

Founded in 1966, RIF is a national nonprofit organization with local projects run by volunteers in every state of the union.

Love stories so promising they could only be . . .

MAURA SEGER
Summer Heat

Gavin McClure's appearance on her porch immediately angered Josie Delmar. After a morning of dealing with ranch hands and cattle, she has no time for another city slicker. And, she is no less pleased when she heard *he* was her silent partner—and determined to stay on "their" ranch! Yet when Gavin trades his city image for boots and saddle, Josie finds her heart warming, and his tender kisses and strong arms soon have her growing weaker by the minute . . .

ISBN: 0-517-00804-1 $2.95

Children often play an important part in my stories because they've always been such an essential part of my life. When *Heat Lightning* reaches the bookstores it will be March and spring, and our youngest child's birthday will be just around the corner. Christopher was born on a blustery, icy March twenty-first, and I think of him as my harbinger of spring.

Children get under the skin. You'll see snatches of David and Elizabeth, our older two, in other books, but *Heat Lightning* is studded with glimpses of Christopher's personality. It is also the story of a father who is as close to his child as my husband, Clyde, is to our children. And it is the story of a woman who comes to love the child as much as she loves the child's father. Linked with love are fear of loss and the willingness to forgive.

I hope you enjoy *Heat Lightning*.

Kathleen Eagle